# Love
# Challenge

Written By: Carrie Farley

Love Challenge

Copyright © 2021 by Beauty From Ashes, LLC

ISBN: 978-0-578-90522-8

# Dedication and Acknowledgements

I will ALWAYS thank **God** for allowing me to continue in this writing thing! Lord, I do not take this gift for granted and pray that I always lift you up in whatever endeavor I choose to pursue.

**Frances Marr, aka "Mommie Dearest,"** I thank you for your continued support and encouragement to finish this third book. The unwavering loyalty towards helping me shine, no one can EVER begin to match...you are forever the "Wind Beneath My Wings." I thank God for your life and, most importantly, your love. "You only get one..."

To the hubby, **Jermaine Farley**, and our children....**Jordynn and Calynn**...thank you so much for your patience, understanding, and unconditional support while I was grinding to get this project done. From the late nights up writing and no "family night," to eating quick meals sometimes; because I was on a deadline... Thank God for you guys. I pray one day, this hobby will begin to lay a foundation for added blessings and opportunities for our family.

To my Pastor, **Apostle William A. Lash III** of the City of Victory Church, I thank you for your support and for making me speak for ten and fifteen minutes at a time during Sunday morning services. The messages I had to prepare to teach have given me some of the content to use in my stories. Not only have you encouraged me to step out of my comfort zone, but you are helping me grow stronger in my faith and confidence in speaking in front of others.

My BFF since 1st grade, **Janneseka Franklin, aka "Nese,"** and my Cousin, **Alyssa Moseley**....THANK YOU for the editing and late nights. I was up reading this to you. Gathering your opinions on how the flow of the story was going. I appreciate your commitment to being a sounding board and voice of reason. Gregory Champion, thanks for the assistance also, fam.

****This Love Series will always be dedicated to my father, the late and great **Boyde L. Marr**...**Forever a "Daddy's Girl."*****

**\*Last, but DEFINITELY not least, I would like to acknowledge those who have supported this series so far. Whether it was from buying both copies, sharing a post, or telling someone else about the books...You are appreciated... I hope you enjoy Love Challenges!**

# Love

# Challenge

# Aftermath

Sunlight began to creep in Ondrea's living room at her condo. It was around eight o'clock in the morning. Bria sat up straight from her position on the couch where she slept that night. Her heart went out to her friend of over fifteen years—who seemed like she just couldn't catch a break. Bria then went down the hall to Ondrea's bedroom to peek in on her and make sure she had not woken back up. Bria then proceeded to check her phone to see if Dearron had called yet. Still, the only message she had was a text from Tyrin telling her he was on his way to see about Ondrea and bringing one of his homemade breakfast pizzas.

*"No, he didn't,"* Bria said as she hurried to spruce herself up in the guest bathroom before Tyrin got there. Aside from being fearless, fine, and great in bed, he also was a good cook. It had been years since Bria had been

privileged to sample his food. Still, she knew whatever

Tyrin made—especially her favorite—pizza, was going to

hit the spot. She was too excited to see him and for them to

be alone in the same space. *"Don't be getting excited...*

*girl, you are married!"* Bria chastised herself as she picked

her phone back up to shoot 'D a text to see when he would

be coming to pick her up from Ondrea's so that they could

head back home. Simultaneously, she felt her phone vibrate

again to another text from Tyrin saying he had just pulled

up.

****

The front door opened where Tyrin stood, revealing

his former flame Bria. They had been through so much

together, and Tyrin did not trust too many females, let

alone allow them to get close to him. He had referenced her

as his soulmate, although she married another guy from

high school—Dearron Howard. *"Sure, dude polished her*

*up...got her laced... he's saved, preaches and all, but I'm the only one who can please her...who really knows her..."* he snapped out of the rant in his head. Soul ties are a motha.

"What's up 'Breeze'?" he asked as she grabbed the breakfast pizza from him.

"Hey," she sang as she danced into Ondrea's kitchen to get first dibs on the grub and tried to ignore the pet name he made up for her the last time they had been intimate before he went to prison.

"So, how's my family?" he asked sincerely.

"Well, Tania wanted to finish her birthday weekend up with Londyn, so the worst part we don't have to deal with yet..."

"True...and 'Drea?"

"She was still sleeping when I checked on her a little while ago...so..." Bria started to change the subject, "...how are you doing?"

Tyrin's jaw twitched, and his vein was starting to pop out of his neck, and that's when Bria knew he was still raging mad.

"I'm trying to calm myself down; I mean, I could've killed that nigga if he hadn't of took off when I pulled my gun."

Bria put her slice of pizza down, walked around the counter to him and began to slowly rub his back in a circular motion three times, and stroked his cheek. She always knew how to calm him down.

"'Rin, you know you can't risk getting into any more trouble. You're finally legit. Your son is in a good school...you got your businesses doing well. If you get locked back up, 'T is gonna need you…Taylor is gonna need you…"

"What about you? You need me?" Tyrin stared into her eyes, searching her soul for the answer he'd always hoped for.

"You're gonna always be my 'Superman,' 'Rin," Bria said before looking away from him, "but we both know I can't belong to you. 'D is my husband, and I'm happy…and Taylor is happy with you…"

"But I'm not happy, Bria…" Tyrin held her chin to turn her face back towards his. "With Taylor or any other chick, I'm 'Mr.-Feel-Good,' and that's it…I'm not happy," he stated again firmly as he grabbed Bria and pulled her into him, kissing her.

Caught off guard by his response, Bria kissed him back. Tyrin continued kissing her as he lifted her up on top of the kitchen counter. Still, before things could go any

further, they heard movement coming from inside Ondrea's

master bedroom.

"This conversation ain't over, Breeze," Tyrin said

matter-of-factly, releasing Bria from his hold.

Both Bria and Tyrin began to walk towards

Ondrea's room to check on her. *"Thank You, Lord, for that*

*way of escape…I don't want to keep disappointing You and*

*messing up in this marriage,"* she prayed to herself. Bria

loved Dearron with all her heart, but the hold that Tyrin had

on her was so strong. The fact that he stopped her from

being brutally raped years ago never left her memory…in

so many ways, she felt indebted to him.

****

Bria gently knocked on the door before coming in,

"Hey cow, it's me."

Ondrea was just getting back into the bed when Bria walked in. She really didn't know why she was standing there in her room. More importantly, Tyrin was there also and standing alongside Bria.

"Hey...what are you two doing at my place?" Ondrea asked suspiciously.

Both Tyrin and Bria looked at each other with a puzzled look on their faces. *"She must have blacked last night out,"* Tyrin thought. "How are you feeling, Cuzzo? I had to carry you and get you home last night," he asked.

"I don't know. I had this terrible dream just now, and I woke up and went to the restroom to gather my composure."

"Well, what was the dream?" Bria asked curiously.

"It's so disturbing, I don't even want to say… 'Rin and Kamal were fighting each other, Kamal's real name was 'Ice,' and somehow, he was responsible for Chance's murder," she finished.

Bria immediately began to comfort Ondrea with a big hug while looking up at Tyrin to confirm. He cleared his throat:

"Unfortunately, 'Drea, that wasn't a dream. I meant to kill him."

"But I don't understand," said Ondrea confused, "I thought you guys were starting to get cool with each other at Tania's surprise…'"

"…Yeah, but that's when I found out 'Big Cash's boy was Kamal, who also used to go by 'Ice' in the life… That's why I never fooled with him from jump…I knew it was something up with him."

"I know he had a past before he gave his life to Christ, 'Rin…it doesn't add up…"

"His people killed Chance, 'Drea. Your boy organized the whole hit because his people was killed… 'Ice' was at Chance because he thought Chance killed ole' boy from their set."

Ondrea remembered that night like it was yesterday. When Chance told her that he was worried because Tyrin owed some people money, and when one of their members began to threaten Tyrin's life, one of Chance's men took his gun, murdering one of their rival members.

"No, no, no, no, no…" Ondrea's tears started forming in her eyes. "You're lying just because you don't like him, 'Rin, and that's not cool."

There's no way that God would allow the man that she loved to be responsible for the death of her first love, husband, and her best friend. Ondrea looked to Bria for confirmation for what she knew to be true. "Tell me he's lying..." Ondrea pleaded with her eyes. By the way, Bria went to hug her again—this time even tighter. She knew Tyrin wasn't lying.

****

After comforting her and Ondrea, assuring them that she was okay to be left alone until Tania returned, Tyrin left with Bria following behind about an hour later after Dearron picked her up to head back to Savannah in time for service in the morning. They all decided it was best if Tania did not know about last night's events—that Pandora's box did not need to be opened.

Ondrea lay down across her bed, still trying to process the bombshell that had been dropped on her heart, exploding, and leaving it—once again, shattered in a million pieces. She fidgeted with her engagement ring while her phone began to ring. It was Kamal calling for the ninth time since the early morning. She couldn't talk to him right now. She then checked her text messages...all thirteen of them were from him as well. **Blocked**.

Ondrea proceeded to get down off her bed and kneeled down to do the only thing she knew how to do. *"Lord, I'm speechless...I don't even understand."* As she began her

conversation with God, she began to weep hysterically, clutching her pillow. *"My heart hurts... I need You..."* Ondrea managed to say in between her cries and sniffles... *"Jesus, I need You...I need You!!!!"*

****

He was grateful for his friend, Dearron, making sure he could leave the scene last night safe and pray with him this morning before he and Bria left to head back home.

Kamal paced back and forth on the balcony of his apartment, checking his phone. He then saw his text messages change from the color blue to green. **"Not delivered."** Kamal then knew he was blocked. He was sick to his stomach. *"Lord, I can't believe this. I know that what we sow, we reap…but I never thought the trade-off would be her broken heart for mine."* A single tear started to stream down his face as he began to flashback on that horrific period in his life.

Left cold-hearted from the hand that he was dealt in life, Kamal Anthony Davis, aka "Ice," did not stop at anything to get to the top, becoming one of the biggest distributors in the state of Georgia. On the road to money, power, and respect, "Ice" had already eliminated four of the most notorious gangsters. Still, there was one who was at his crew, and he had to be stopped.

Kamal knew "Fate" was not the one who pulled the trigger and killed his best friend that night; however, he knew that if he wanted his crew to take over, he needed to take out the competition. "Fate" was one of the most respected and feared guys in the street. Kamal put a $10K bounty on his head, sat back, and waited for someone to deliver his competition to him, dead or alive. After his successful attempt and rise to fame, he had thought that situation was behind him. Never in his wildest dreams did Kamal imagine the very "fate" he'd deal with once he became saved was with his "chance" for trying to secure a future with his fiancée' after she learned he had something to do with her husband's murder. *"I didn't know his name was Chance...Lord if I am Your manservant...if I am called of You and can now hold up clean and Holy hands in Your presence, Lord, You have to make this right for me! Lord, I ask that You minister to my Ondrea, Lord! I ask that You speak to her heart and let her know. I did not know—even though it still doesn't erase what damage was done. I thank*

*and praise You in advance for the victory already, in your*

*Son, Jesus' name I pray, Amen and Amen."*

# Chapter One

"So, you really told him while he was bringing you home?!" squealed Tania jumping up and down with excitement, trying not to drop her iPhone. She hoped this was a sign that Londyn was going to keep her baby with 'T.

"I had no choice but to tell him, sis…I threw up all night after you and Sebastian left."

"Congrats on the niece or nephew, brat!" Sebastian interjected while interrupting the best friends' Facetime gossip.

"Anyways, Londyn…continue before we were rudely interrupted!" Tania said as she flipped her high-end ponytail in Sebastian's face and gave him a playful nudge. He then, in return, smacked her on the butt and went back into their hotel room. "So…. spill the beans, heffa!"

"He was like, 'What?!' and then, after about a minute later, he started smiling and asked me if I would keep it. That smile and the sparkle in those blue eyes of his… I couldn't tell your cousin no," Londyn sighed.

"That's the problem," Tania said jokingly.

"Too soon, heffa," Londyn replied while rolling her eyes, "Now, we have to find a way to let our parents know…" her voice trailed off with great worry.

"I know…how about writing your mom and dad a letter…T might have to tell his dad on the phone and not in person, though…"

"That's what I was afraid of... I was hoping he would not want to keep the baby, so we could have avoided this part."

Although she loved T, she had already planned for having a "normal" life and having a baby with him would just complicate things. Furthermore, Londyn was already being critiqued and criticized "constructively" by her parents daily. There was always something she should be doing, be better in or about, or doing more of while scaling back on others.

"Babies are blessings…focus on that. I can't wait to spoil my niece or nephew and have them wearing all kinds of cute fits…plus, look on the bright side… it may slow T down from hanging with those no-good friends of his now…you never know why things happen the way that they do."

"I hear you, sis, but if they are that much of a blessing, then why don't you and Sebastian have one, then?"

"Because that's not my path. Quiet as kept, day-to-day, I don't know if we're even going to make it, so I'm definitely not giving up my goodies."

"I hear you—wait, you mean to tell me last night you two spent the night together, and nothing happened?"

"Don't get me wrong, third base was still on and cracking, plus I gave him a 'one-time for the one-time' for still being patient with me."

"Girl!"

"I know!" Tania exclaimed. "I'm NOT doing that anymore," she laughed.

"What you not gonna do no more, babe?" Sebastian asked as he snuck up behind Tania. He wanted to try his luck again at connecting with her.

Tania took time to inhale his Vera Wang cologne and felt Sebastian's hardness. She turned around to look at him and the sensual look in his light brown eyes and knew what was next. She hung up with Londyn and began kissing him. They made it to the bed, and as soon as he pulled out a condom, Tania tensed up again. She thought to herself, *"Jesus, I can't do this…Dang, my little outfit from HER Curves Boutique is banging too…God, why you make me so sensitive to Your Spirit like this!"*

Sebastian could feel Tania tensing up on him as he was planting kisses up and down her body. He wanted this moment to be unique between them and not worry about the ramifications afterward. He sighed to himself, *"I might as well just stop while I'm ahead because it's not gonna happen, dude."* He got up from the bed.

"Sebastian, babe, where are you going?!" Tania jumped up, demanding. She knew something was wrong, and she was starting to get nervous.

He turned around to face his girlfriend, "Babe, I know you ain't ready still to make this happen, so I'm stopping it now…I'm about to take a cold shower."

"I'm so sorry, babe…I-I'm… Please don't be mad with me," Tania pleaded, looking at him in his eyes longingly.

Tania was relieved but also worried about what this meant for the two of them. She knew Sebastian had the hotel room rented to celebrate her birthday. They talked about it for several weeks now. She wanted to oblige him, but there was doubt in the back of Tania's mind that she and Sebastian would not be together always. Both her mother and Minister Kamal taught Tania. They told her that her virginity was priceless and was to mean everything to her. She was not to give it to anyone that would not be her husband. More importantly, God would not be pleased.

"It's okay, Tania," Sebastian lied. He did not want her to know how much he was disappointed with how things turned out. He had gone through a lot to set everything up, not to mention spent a good amount that he had saved up for their night. "We're good, babe," Sebastian added as he got out of the shower to dry off. "Just promise me you'll let me know when you're down," he said with a smile and a wink.

# Chapter Two-

Ondrea's alarm went off. 7:00 AM. It was Sunday morning, and time for her to get up and get ready for church. *"I don't think I want to see him right now…it's too soon,"* she thought. *"Tania would probably be there and wonder where I am... I'll just tell her I'm not feeling well—that wasn't a lie, right, Lord?"* Ondrea rolled back over in her bed and drifted back off to sleep.

****

By the time Tania pulled into the parking lot and got out of her new car with Londyn, they could hear the church getting their praise on all the way outside. Destiny to Faith Ministries was Marietta, Georgia's best-kept secret. A small church that was mighty in faith and packed with power were the ingredients to the ministry's success and the overall spiritual well-being of the members in their congregation.

"Dang, we missed Sunday School!" lamented Londyn.

"I know, right...On a brighter note, maybe you can go up for prayer to cure yourself of that morning sickness, sis."

"I'm thinking about it, strongly," stated Londyn. "I'm just worried, Minister Davis would pick up that I'm pregnant when I come up for prayer," she said as they walked up the steps to the front door.

"Girl, you oughta know by now, if God is gonna show him something, you know it won't matter whether you come up for prayer or not!"

"You're right—he's always on point...guess I might as well get this prayer for my nausea, then."

Once inside, both girls caught a glimpse of Sincere Phillips, one of Mother Helen's grandsons, who just so happened to be visiting this Sunday.

"Girl, look!" exclaimed Londyn. "That brotha knows he's fine...if Sebastian acts up, you know Sincere can get that act right!" she added.

"Girl, I don't know what you're talking about, sis!" Tania retorted. "He ain't checking for me..."

"Every girl in this church knows he's at you, Tania."

"Whatever." Tania made sure she put a switch in her hips as she sashayed down the aisle in a cute, maroon-colored dress she had purchased from Shein. She could feel Sincere's eyes watching her as she and Londyn made their way to their usual seats together. She wondered why he was here, but Mother Helen wasn't anywhere in sight.

Before Kamal got up to preach, the church secretary announced that Mother Helen had been taken to the hospital earlier that morning and to keep her in prayer for a speedy recovery.

Mother Helen was like an extended family member to Ondrea and her step-father-to-be. Tania pulled out her iPhone immediately. She wanted to make sure that she got the information to her mother ASAP.

****

With the combination of Friday night's events and Ondrea still not responding to him in addition to the recent news about Mother Helen, Kamal was struggling to hold onto the faith that he would be able to even deliver a message to his congregation this morning. He glanced over at Tania and her friend. He never knew that his actions sixteen years ago would cause his future daughter-in-law to have had to grow up with the void of not having a father. *"Not by my power, or might, but by Your Spirit, Lord, come in and take control. Your strength is made perfect in my weakness, "* he prayed to himself. He needed God to intervene as he stepped up to the podium. He within himself was depleted.

"I must say to everyone that I need you to pray this morning like never before…the devil is busy, but Christ came so that we may have life and have it more abundantly."

"Amen!" Brother Bryan called out.

After Kamal had given the honor, he continued. "I'd like to take my thought from Ephesians 6:10-20… 'Clothed and In My Right Mind.'"

"Take your time, Pastor!" someone shouted.

"In the natural, when we think about putting our clothes on, we think of the normal items: shirt, pants, underwear, socks, and/or shoes. Depending on the weather, you might even wear protective gear such as a hat or a coat. Now, suppose you happened to go outside and see someone walking down the street without any clothes. In that case, the first thing you are going to think is, 'have they lost their mind?' and get uncomfortable if they even tried to approach us in that state.

Even stores will not even provide service to you if you aren't wearing a shirt or shoes." Some people began to snicker in the congregation.

"There are some who may get offended by those types of signs; however, the store owners aren't judging those who are offended because, in all actuality, clothing is made for our skin's covering and protection...if we don't wear our protective gear and it starts raining out of nowhere, or its ice on the ground after a good snow, and you slip and fall...hindsight kicks in and you are like, 'I should've brought that umbrella,' or even better—ladies, you think you should have just worn your boots instead of your heels, but you still mad though."

"You are talking right, Pastor!" Shouted out another female member, while some of the others agreed in laughter.

"So, when we think spiritually, there's too many of us Christians—I included at times—who walk around without everything on and want to get upset when something happens. It could be an attack from the enemy or something that I caused to bring upon myself, but this is the equivalent of not having the proper clothing or protective gear on."

"Come on now!" shouted out another member.

"In case you may not know the proper 'clothing' to wear in Christ, the blueprint is right here in Ephesians," Kamal added as he held his Bible up in the air. "First, God tells us to wear the belt of truth. Wearing this means knowing the Word of God and believing that He is King of all Kings and Lord of all Lords and that through His son, Jesus Christ, we are saved."

"Talk about that resurrecting power!" shouted Londyn's father.

"To wear the breastplate of righteousness means that you believe this Word and Christ with all of your heart. To fully understand Him, you must acknowledge Him wholeheartedly. Then, and only then can you walk in truth and have the confidence in Him that we should. Next, He said to put on your shoes of the gospel of peace. This means being humble and not seeking after worldly possessions or evils. When we step on the scene, and there's chaos, the atmosphere should command peace and love when we're in the midst. Remembering that everywhere we step is Holy Ground will help us to stay focused—no matter the environment."

Kamal felt his help coming from the Holy Spirit. He was ready for take-off.

"Speaking of environments, when you are carrying your shield of faith, we must remember that we are fighting a good fight of faith and that we should never doubt or deny God's power that he possesses to work every situation out—if it is His Will. No weapon formed against me and mine shall prosper! That shield represents the blocks that you have to hit against those negative thoughts, ideas, and images that come to you in your mind.... those impure thoughts...When the enemy comes up against us, the Lord will lift up the standard—you have to make this personal so that your faith can work for you...for without faith it is impossible to please Him...impossible!"

"Jesus," Londyn's mother cried out.

"Wearing that helmet of salvation, again, just reiterates knowing without a shadow of a doubt that you are saved. No one or nothing will be able to separate you from the love of Christ. The last part of your Christian uniform is the accessory of a sword. This is also the equivalent of a gun. The tongue is like a two-edged sword, and when you speak nothing but God's Word, demons must flee! In the name of Jesus!"

"Thank you, Jesus!" a woman in the congregation began screaming and shouting down the aisle way and back.

"Praise Him, Sister!" Kamal encouraged the woman that was getting her breakthrough. "You have the protective gear…never leave home without it…and that's prayer. This, Church, is only activated after we have put on everything else that God told us to wear. Prayer helps us to keep our armor intact so that if we face one of those long and hard battles, we'll be able to stand until deliverance comes. Some were healed as they went, and others instantly. It didn't matter when they were healed, though…what matters is that they had the faith, patience, and prayer life to weather the storm until their healing came…pray without ceasing, Saints! Joy comes in the morning!"

"Hallelujah!" cried out another member as they too began to shout. Next, the entire congregation began shouting and praising God after being encouraged and uplifted by God's

Word that was brought forth.

****

"There he is, sis...he's coming this way...look!" Londyn said to Tania with excitement as Sincere, who stood tall at 6'5," started making his way over to the both of them after service was over.

Tania smiled and secretly hoped that her ponytail was still in place from shouting earlier in service, and her breath was not stale. *He is so fine*, she thought to herself. While she preferred the lighter complexion of her boo— Sebastian and the way he grew and styled his "man-bun," it was something about Sincere's smooth and flawless brown skin, hair with waves that made you sea-sick (thanks to his barber, Timon Pitts) all the way down to the nose ring he had. No one has been able to successfully pull that off since the late, great Tupac Shakur. He was looking sophisticated and sexy in a grey and blue suit from Jos. A. Bank with the matching belt and navy blue Cole Haans.

"Good morning, ladies," Sincere said, smiling while he flashed his pearly whites.

"Morning, Sincere," they both replied in unison.

"We're sorry to hear about your grandmother. We are definitely praying." Tania added sincerely.

"Thank you so much. Our grandma is the matriarch of our family. I had to come down from Philly to see what's going on."

"How long are you in town?" Londyn asked.

"I don't know yet...I'm just glad our first quarter just ended," he added. Although he was seventeen, Sincere was a first-year engineering student-athlete at Temple University. By him being so accomplished as a student-athlete playing college ball, on top of knowing he was from the East Coast, every teenage girl at church wanted his attention and believed that they could pull him—except, he only seemed to have eyes for Miss Williams.

"Okay, well, if you or your family need anything, make sure you let us know while you're here," replied Londyn, nudging Tania.

"Oh—yeah, let me write down my number if you ever need to talk…you know, as a friend," Tania said as she wrote her number down on the back of her church bulletin.

"Thanks so much, you two," Sincere replied while bending down to hug Londyn in response. "I'll be sure to call," He turned towards Tania and extended his arms open to her.

While Tania returned the hug back, she found herself not wanting him to let her go. *I definitely should not be lusting after this boy, especially in Your house, God. I am so sorry… why'd you have to make him so fine, Lord?* She joked to herself.

****

"Tania!" Kamal waved and called out to his future daughter—or so he hoped.

"Hey, 'Dad,'" she replied with a hug and a smile. Tania loved the fact that her spiritual

father was also going to have the natural father role in her life. She had longed for a father for so long. All Tania had left of her real father, Chance, were pictures that her mother had given her, along with her stuffed teddy bear, "Snookie." He had won for her at a carnival shortly before he was murdered. "Great service, as per usual...mom texted me and said she wasn't feeling well. I know you probably know already, but just in case..."

"No, Tania, I didn't, but thanks for letting me know."

That was rather odd seeing that both were together when she, Londyn, and T left her birthday event—not to mention how much her mom and Minister Kamal stayed on the phone together. "Did you and my mom get into an argument or beef or something?" she asked.

*I wonder how much she knows.* Kamal questioned. "I did make her a little upset, but we're good, Tania," he spoke in faith.

"Okay…" she replied playfully. "I need ya'll to make it to that altar, so this will be official, Dad…I want a little sister or brother soon," she smiled and winked.

"Whoa, slow down, little lady!" he replied with shock. "We haven't even decided if we want any more children."

"Well, I'm deciding for you. Plus, Jonoah needs a playmate when you guys all link up for the annual family vacays or something. I'm speaking it into existence!" said Tania while playfully nudging Minister Kamal and taking off to catch back up with Londyn.

*That went well...thank You, Lord!* Kamal went back into his office, sat down in his chair, and pulled out his iPhone in another attempt to try to get in contact with Ondrea. It went straight to her voicemail. Feeling defeated, Kamal hung up without leaving a message. He then shot a text message to Dearron, inquiring what he might have been able to find out from his wife, Bria, on Ondrea's mental state.

He responded: **"What's up, bro! So far, she's [Ondrea] still in shock. We're praying for the both of you to get through this. God is faithful, my friend. Remember, we're here."**

# Chapter Three-

Ondrea heard Tania's car alarm and immediately sprang up from the couch in her pink Chanel sweats and ran back into her bedroom—shutting the door behind her. Ondrea was not ready to see anyone right now, let alone look her daughter in the face. Her daughter was a reminder of the love both she and Chance shared. Her one and only. *Just when I find another man who can even start to take that place in my heart and life again, I find out he's responsible for Chance's murder? This is some kind of sick joke...*

Hey mom," Tania called out as she entered her mother's condo.

"Hey, my headache," Ondrea called back. *Please don't come in here,* she wished.

Tania knocked on her mother's bedroom door, "Are you feeling any better, Mom?" she asked, turning the knob slowly as she entered her room.

Ondrea sat up in her bed, quickly composing herself, "I'm fine, darling, just a slight headache."

Tania looked closely at her mother, who was in her Chanel sweats—meaning something was wrong. Legend had it that she wore the same outfit when she found out about her father being murdered.

"Mom, what's wrong? Did you and Dad have a fight or something, and that's the real reason you didn't come to church today?"

*She is too intelligent*, thought Ondrea. "He's not your 'father' yet, Tania…but anyway, we had a disagreement of some sorts, but nothing for you to worry your pretty little self over."

"Alright, all I know is I want nothing in the way of you two getting married this Thanksgiving…I told him I want a brother or sister, too."

"You what?!" Ondrea yelled.

"Dang, mom—" Tania said, startled.

"I-I'm sorry, baby…I was just taken by surprise, that's all…there is NO way on God's precious green Earth that I would have another baby…do you know how old I am?"

"Whatever, Mom...He doesn't have any kids of his own, just give him one baby, and I'll watch it all the time…better than me having one," she added playfully.

"Alright now, don't make me whoop your butt!" replied Ondrea throwing one of the decorative pillows at Tania that was on her bed. *I'm glad he didn't tell her what happened.*

Tania moved out the way, just in time before the pillow hit her body and fell onto the floor instead. "Oh, Mom, did you get my text earlier about Mother Helen being in the hospital?" she asked, changing the subject.

"No, I haven't checked my phone yet...what's wrong?" Ondrea asked while bracing herself for the worse.

"She was taken to the emergency room early this morning. They didn't announce any

more details as to why but just asked everyone to pray for her."

Ondrea became nervous, "Did they say what hospital she was in?"

"I can find out if you still don't want to talk to him right now," Tania added supportively.

"No, thank you, baby…I'll go on ahead and reach out to him. It's about Mother Helen and not about us right now."

****

Kamal was lying across the couch in his living room area. He enjoyed watching the Cleveland Browns play his Atlanta Falcons when he heard the notification that he had received a text message. The picture Ondrea took of both of them the night that they kissed popped up. *It's her!* Kamal hurried to retrieve the message:

**"Praise the Lord, Minister. I am wondering if you know which hospital Mother Helen was taken to, and if so, can you send me the location, please, and thanks in advance."**

He sighed with frustration. It wasn't the text message he had hoped to receive from Ondrea, but at the same time, Kamal was glad for any type of interaction from her at this point.

**"Sure, Lady. Whatever you need. Mother Helen is at Kennestone Cancer Center."**

**"Thanks for the quick response, Minister Kamal."**

Kamal quickly replied to see if he could continue their conversation: **"Not delivered."** *Dang, It's back to 'Minister Kamal' now?!* He felt anger and anxiety trying to creep in and quickly rebuked the thoughts. *Lord, in Your name! I thank You for a breakthrough somewhere with Ondrea and me. Jesus, heal her heart and minister unto her how deeply I am sorry for the hurt and pain I have caused in taking away her husband and Tania's father. Lord, help me to be able to forgive myself so that I can once again stand with authority and power in knowing I am still your* *manservant, and most importantly—Your child. In Jesus'*

*name, Amen.*

# Chapter Four-

*Cancer Center? How long has she had it? What kind? Did she know all along?* Ondrea pondered these questions while on her way to the hospital to see Mother Helen. For all Ondrea knew, her Infiniti SUV was not moving fast enough to get her there to the hospital to visit.

"Well, come on in, child…I've been expecting you!" Mother Helen stated as she saw Ondrea peek her head in her hospital room.

Ondrea sat by Mother Helen's bedside. "How are you doing, Mother?" she asked as she took her hand.

"I'm doing just fine. I'm in God's hands…no place better than that, Ondrea. It's Stage 4 colon cancer. I have no pain or anything…God is still good to me, you hear? Now tell me, what's going on with you, honey? You have some things you need to release and get off your chest, daughter."

A wave of emotions came over Ondrea. How did this other mother figure that she had come to know and had grown to love called out specific things going on with her? Her eyes began to well up with tears. Ondrea shook her head no, holding her tears. "It's going to be alright; I just need you to focus on getting better, Mother Helen."

"Hmph…" Mother Helen retorted, "Well, I'm gonna offer my two cents, and you can do what you want with it, honey…how does that sound?"

"Yes, ma'am," Ondrea chuckled a little.

"Things are going to get pretty bad—if they haven't already with you and the Minister. The devil will try and bring up things from his past to try and destroy the plans God has for the both of you in the future. Whatever you do,

Ondrea, you must remember whatever you learn about his past—if it's revealed—that you remember God's deliverance power in his life and that he is not the same man you found out he was in his past."

"Mother, how'd you—"

"Honey, I'm prayed up, and God talks to me!" Mother Helen boasted with a wink and smirk on her face. "Maybe one day, you'll have the pleasure of being close to God in this way. I'm getting a little tired, but remember what I said, and pray, my darling…don't discuss with anyone else…and pray that God reveals your next steps," she then squeezed her hand.

Ondrea squeezed her hand back. "Yes, ma'am, I love you and get some rest," she replied as she kissed Mother Helen on the top of her head and left to head out of the hospital room.

Back in her SUV, Ondrea could not help but smile when she turned on the Kirk Franklin radion station on XM Satellite radio, and Issac Caree's "Good Vibes" show was on. As she blasted the banger "Use Me" by Karla Clay-Alexander, she knew that this was a sign from God that she was supposed to heed Mother Helen's words of wisdom.

# Chapter Five-

Back at school, everyone raved about Tania's birthday bash. Although Tania was happy about the attention she had received, the more pressing issue was that both her best friend, Londyn, and her cousin 'T needed her help. Londyn was almost four months pregnant, and they needed to tell both her parents and her cousin's dad.

"So, 'T…what do you think Cousin Tyrin will say when you tell him?" Tania asked as they all walked towards her car after practice.

"Man, cuz I don't know!" he said.

"Do you think he'll hurt you? "Tania asked.

"I honestly don't know, Tania…You know Pop is crazy, and he doesn't want anything messing with my potential basketball or academic scholarships...I got recruiters already from Duke and USC coming to my games now, and I still have a whole two more years before I graduate high school...Pop is gonna make sure I know I f— 'ed up," he stated.

"Real talk, Cuzzo...do you really see yourself staying with Londyn and being a family with a baby?"

"Tania, I actually do...I know it sounds crazy with all the action I'm used to getting...but what your dad and cousin 'Drea had, I want something like that with your girl—of course not ending tragically with dying as they did..."

Tania couldn't have been prouder of her cousin than she was at this moment. 'T had always been rough around the edges and just needed polishing up to be at the highest level of potential he could be. Londyn and her background helped to challenge that. She really hoped the best for her BFF and cousin.

"I helped Londyn write a letter to her parents, but she's scared to give it to them…maybe the two of you can let them know together—"

"Hell no!" he replied. "I'm not getting jumped by both our dads...that's not about to fly with me, Cuzzo."

Tania sympathized with her older cousin, and at that moment, she could see why they both were scared.

Londyn was already in the front seat, buckled in and waiting for them to all arrive at Ondrea's car. "Y'all, I gotta pee! Hurry up and get in the car!" she exclaimed. She had a thing about using public restrooms and wished 'T's car wasn't in the shop, or she would have just left practice with him. Londyn didn't know how much longer she'd be able to keep cheering before people started to notice her growing belly.

Tania was purposely trying to wait up for Sebastian, who seemed preoccupied conversing with another teammate. Still, she could tell now that she would just have to catch up with him later. She sent him a text that she would go ahead and drop Londyn off and that Tania would call him when she arrived back at her house.

"So, I just came up with a brilliant idea that I shared with 'T. Londyn, how about you guys invite your parents and his dad out somewhere, and you two can share the news in a public setting, and that way, they are less likely to give the reaction that you think they may give?"

Londyn thought long and hard about the proposal. It wasn't necessarily a bad idea, and it would take off some of the pressure from her to tell her parents in private. She knew there was the possibility that she would be subject to who-knows-what kind of insult and ridicule. "I actually like the idea, sis…thanks."

"Hold up, babe…but your dad is gonna kill me, we're not even gonna start with mine—"

"He'll respect you more if we tell them this way, babe…trust me, he is old school."

"Alright," 'T hesitantly agreed to the plan. "So, when are we gonna try and do this? We got the tourney this weekend. Remember…I don't want to be bruised up while playing. Trust me, I know my dad, and he's gonna give it to me good, at least one time (pause)."

Londyn chuckled at the "pause" joke and pulled her mini-Louis Vuitton day planner out from her matching tote bag. "Let me check because I just made an appointment to find out the sex of the baby and want to make sure we tell them before then. How about we invite them out to dinner next Sunday after church …they might be in the "Spirit" still and won't be so upset… 'T, you think you and your dad might want to be my guests and come to church with me next Sunday?"

'T had not stepped foot inside a church since he was seven years old. His father never went. His mother, Lauren, stayed in and out of jail so much when he was younger. She never had the pleasure or opportunity to even try. "I'll see," was all he promised her, but at least he was being honest.

As Londyn gave goodbye hugs to Tania and kissed 'T upon exiting Tania's car, she started to feel hopeful for the first time since she'd found out she was pregnant.

By the time Tania pulled up to Ondrea's condo, Tyrin had already been waiting outside in his Tesla. He saw the both of them arrive together.

"Look at 'Frick and Frack' pulling up...what ya'll into?"

"Nothing, big cuz," stated Tania.

"Yeah, aight, I know ya'll up to something… especially when ya'll two are together it's something else…" he said suspiciously.

"No, Pop...remember my car had to get the new brakes and rotors?"

"Oh yeah, I forgot," Tyrin stated.

"What are you doing here so early?" Tania asked him.

"Dang, nosey! Well, I came by to check on your mother. I know she wasn't feeling too good the other day...just wanted to holler at her."

"You knew about her and Minister Kamal arguing?"

Immediately Tyrin's nostrils started to flare up, and his jaw twitched out of growing anger. He remembered Tania wasn't supposed to know about what happened, so he quickly snapped back to a more calming mental state. "Yeah, but it wasn't anything major," he lied. "I know she had a bad headache, and I was in the neighborhood also...again, just checking up on her—wait a minute, I don't have to explain myself to no kid," he remembered his authority and used it as an opportunity to shut the conversation down.

"Okay, okay, Cousin Tyrin...dang!" Tania replied playfully.

"'T, you might as well hop in with me, so Tania doesn't have to be out driving late."

"Yessir," 'T said, closing Tania's car door, "alright, cuz." he turned and said to Tania as he gave her a quick hug.

"Love you, Cuzzo!" Tania replied.

****

"Sebastian Michael Wilson, answer your phone!" Tania screamed on his voicemail. It had been two hours since she had texted him when they left school. Since Sunday, she had been getting weird vibes from Sebastian, and she couldn't help but pay attention to her gut feeling that he might be itching to scratch or entertain someone else.

Just as she hung up from dialing Sebastian, she received an incoming call from a phone number with a 267-area code. *Who is this?* Tania wondered as she answered, "Hello?"

"Hello, am I speaking to Reginae Carter?"

"Um, I'm sorry to disappoint you, but this isn't her, have a great day—"

"Wait, hold up...don't hang up, Tania," the familiar voice urged.

"Who is this?" she demanded.

"It's Sincere," he laughed, responding back.

"Oh my gosh! Boy, you play too much...Reginae Carter?!" she remained puzzled but returned the laugh.

"She's the closest female that's fire to me right now that I could compare you to—dimples, smile, body, and all."

Tania was blushing at the compliment. "Well,

now…you don't say?" she replied playfully. "So, to what do I owe the pleasure of this phone call?"

Sincere's voice turned severe in that split second, "Well, they're moving my grandmother to Hospice tomorrow, and I wanted to make sure you and your mom knew. I know my grandmother loves your mom…" his voice trailed off.

"Where are you? I can meet you someplace if you need a hug—"

"I'm actually on my way to visit with her. She's starting to transition right now, and I kind of just want to be with her alone…I just needed to know I have a friend who was close by their phone."

"Sincere, I got you…anyways, just call me whenever you need to talk, and I'll make sure I pick up. I'll be praying for you guys and, of course, Mother Helen and her comfort."

"Thanks so much, Tania…I'm glad I did call you."

"Me too," she replied before saying their goodbyes.

*Sebastian better get it together* was all she had to say.

## Chapter Six-

After Tania told Ondrea the news about Mother

Helen, she was too outdone. On Tuesday, Ondrea cleared

her schedule to sit with Mother Helen out at Hospice for

the entire evening —she didn't feel like going to Bible

Study and seeing or dealing with Kamal just yet. She had

been prayerful but now was dreading having to eventually

face the man responsible for taking her husband's

life. Ondrea had put him back on her call block list, and if

it weren't for the situation with Mother Helen, she wouldn't

have decided to remove him today.

Mother Helen looked different this time when

Ondrea saw her. She looked at peace and hardly moved and

couldn't say anything. Sincere and his parents had

previously been out to see her. Mother Helen's other

daughter from North Carolina was expected to fly in at any time now. Ondrea knew today would be the last day that she would see Mother Helen on this side of life.

****

It was now around 6:00pm when Ondrea received a text from Kamal. She reluctantly opened his message:

**"Hello, my apologies for bothering you, but can you please tell me how Mother Helen is doing?"** Kamal texted her.

**"Hey, Kamal… she isn't responsive at all…I'm scared…are you on the way? You may want to cancel Bible Study to come and pray with her,"** Ondrea truthfully replied.

**"Okay, just wait right there. I'm coming to you, Lady."** Kamal jumped in his Cadillac SUV and sped all the way to Hospice. Ondrea needed him, and he wasn't going to let the opportunity go by to connect with her.

When Kamal pulled up and walked up to the door to the entrance, he met Ondrea's blank stare and glossy eyes. He knew she was getting ready to break down. As soon as she saw Kamal's face, she allowed her tears to fall. Kamal ran up in time to wrap her up in a big embrace and let her cry in his arms. She was relieved and confused at the same time. How could his presence bring comfort, yet at the same time, he had caused her so much pain?

"Why is all of this happening, Kamal?" she asked, pulling away from his embrace.

"I don't know, Lady…God only knows. I'm going in to pray with her now. Would you like to come with me?"

"I can't go back in there, Kamal…I can't—"

"—it's okay, I understand, Ondrea," he said, cutting her off to save her from admitting her vulnerability. "Can you wait for me to finish praying with her then, and maybe we can go someplace and talk?"

"I don't think that is a good idea, Kamal…I'm not ready to talk tonight."

"Okay, no pressure…just promise me you'll text me when you're ready?"

"I can do that," Ondrea nodded in reply.

As she walked away, and he went inside to Mother Helen's room, he prayed:

*Lord, I thank You for a breakthrough, and I thank You for allowing Ondrea to reach out to me and agree to meet with me at the opportune time and divine appointment. I am continually trusting in and only You to repair and restore our relationship so that we can still move forward in marriage. I thank You in advance for what You have done already in the past, what You've allowed in this present moment, and for what You have in store for my future. I know this is but a mere chapter in my book of life, but again, I give You all the honor and glory. In Jesus' name, I pray, Amen.*

****

Ondrea sat in her car for over fifteen minutes, trying to process the encounter she had just had with Kamal. She started to call Bria, but then Mother Helen's words of wisdom came back to her:

**"He is not the same man  you found out he was in his past…pray, my darling…"**

Ondrea closed her eyes and began to pray: *Lord, I'm coming to You as sincere as it gets. You said to ask. You a hard thing. This is HARD. Part of me never wants to see this man again, while the other wanted to stay in his arms and continue pouring out my tears on his sweater. I am open to whatever You would have me do concerning Kamal and me. Lord, I love him and hate him at the same time. I hate him for what he did and love him for how he has come into my life to rectify all of that hurt and pain. I'm so confused. I'm afraid. I feel so betrayed. Hold me, Lord, and keep me in Your presence. I don't know why You're allowing all of this to occur, but I'm grateful*

*anyhow. In Jesus' name, Amen.*

She then pulled out her phone and texted Kamal: **"Hey, I was doing some thinking, and I can meet you at your place in an hour."**

**\*\*\*\***

At 8:00pm, Kamal read the text message he had gotten from Ondrea, and his heart skipped a beat. *Lord, You work miracles. Thank You but help me to be in order when I talk with her. I don't want to act or speak out of perfect timing. In Your name…*

He pulled up in his complex and immediately spotted her SUV parked next to his parking spot. Kamal gulped as he thought he would have time to get situated and be prayed up further before Ondrea arrived. As she got out of her car and began walking towards him, he became more nervous. He proceeded to lead her up to his apartment.

"You know you are such a special lady for me to let you in my place this late," he said.

"This is the only time you can catch me this week, so it was either take it or leave it," Ondrea stated as she walked inside.

She took notice of Kamal's studio apartment. Although everything was contemporary and modern, she now knew why he was uncomfortable with her spending time with him at his place with it being such close quarters. She walked over to his couch in the television area and sat down in his recliner.

"Impressive," she stated dryly.

Kamal stood over top of her to offer her Perrier water. "Here you go, in case you are thirsty."

"Thank you," she replied.

"Ondrea, will you let me explain what actually happened…I owe you that much."

She hesitantly let out a huge sigh and replied. "I'm listening…" Ondrea put the water down and folded her arms in a defensive stance.

"I did not know that Chance was 'Fate.' All I knew was that someone killed my best friend and that someone from his crew still owed me money…again, I never knew about Chance—just "Fate… I didn't know Tyrin was the one who owed the money, nor did I know anything else."

Ondrea thought back to when she had first met Chance, and his license plate had read "FATE." She looked back up at Kamal. She wanted this to be an easy fix. She wanted to believe that he was being straight-up and honest with her.

"I appreciate you explaining what actually happened. We both know you can't go back and change it, so let's just talk about something else now."

"Well, again, I appreciate you giving me the time to share that with you. I've missed you…how have you been?

She cut her eyes at him in a glare that if looks could kill, Kamal would have been dead. "How do you think I've been, Kamal? Huh? I find out that you had something to do with Chance's murder…how do you think I've been doing?!"

"Okay, okay…I probably should not have asked you that question—"

Ondrea jumped up out of the recliner and in Kamal's face, "You're damn right! Nigga, you have a lot of nerve—"

Shocked and understanding her rage all at the same time, Kamal calmly stepped back to prevent him from automatically swinging back on her if she hit him. He did not want to slip back into "Ice," who didn't care who disrespected him. This woman—he loved. "Ondrea, calm down...we should pray—" he grabbed her arm.

"I don't wanna pray, Kamal...I want things to go back to how they were before I found out you're a fucking murderer!" she yelled, jerking away from him.

"Ondrea, shut up! —" he said back at her; he had heard enough.

"Who the hell do you think you're talking to like that, Kamal? Oh, so you just flip like that cause I called you out, huh? So, you gonna murder me now, huh?! Murderer?!" she smacked him hard across his face.

Kamal's fists clenched as he took her slaps four more times, and then he couldn't take it anymore. He grabbed her up, shaking her while simultaneously backing her up into the wall. "Woman, you better chill! Now, look, Ondrea...I love you...I'm sorry I hurt you, and I can't say that shit enough even if I had ten thousand tongues...deadass!" He looked into her eyes so seriously.

It was in that moment when he threw his calling to the side to bring her back from that dark place that she knew he was being totally one-hundred percent honest with her. Ondrea broke down once again in his arms, weeping uncontrollably. The scent of his Jimmy Choo cologne smelled so good. As she looked up into his eyes, Kamal shedding some tears of his own grabbed her in a light chokehold, and began to kiss her aggressively. Ondrea surrendered to his kisses. His tongue slid into her mouth as both their hands started touching and grabbing everywhere they could. He then stepped back away from her as he felt himself swelling about to burst through his zipper on his pants.

"You don't play any games, do you, Kamal?" Ondrea asked, staring down at his print.

"Whose, Kamal?" he returned while biting his bottom lip, sending tingles straight to Ondrea that she hadn't felt in a while. At this moment, she knew he wasn't Minister Kamal Davis...he was someone else.

Kamal took his shirt off and threw it across the room, exposing a tattoo on the front of his chest and a muscular, chocolate body with six-pack abs. Ondrea cleared her throat as she took her shawl off, revealing her nude-colored tank-style Fashion Nova jumpsuit. He smiled in approval at the tight fit on her slim-thick frame.

"Leave that outfit on, I'll take care of it...turn that thing around for me though," he directed her.

Ondrea obeyed and turned around. She was intrigued by this other side of Kamal and couldn't wait to see how he put it down on her. Kamal then unbuckled his belt, taking it off, and playfully hit Ondrea on her butt with it before throwing it down on the floor. Ondrea was so turned on that she moaned faintly when she felt the belt come across her buttocks. He then removed his pants, revealing the considerably large bulge trapped in his underwear. Ondrea turned back around when she heard Kamal drop his pants. *Whoa, I don't think I'm ready for all those inches,* she thought to herself.

He then motioned for her to come towards him— already calculating his next move. He then began kissing her again. This time…so sensual and slow… to the point Ondrea was throbbing. She then started begging Kamal to be inside her. Kamal bent down, peeling her jumpsuit down while caressing her everywhere he could. Without warning, he picked Ondrea up, kissing her non-stop while he carried her over to the bed. He then pinned her down and proceeded to place his face in between her legs. Ondrea moaned over and over until she almost couldn't breathe. Just when she thought he was finished, Kamal flipped her over and began massaging her until he got to the small of her back. He then began to plant small kisses and flicked his tongue lightly across her lower back until he got to her butt. He then spread her legs wide and began licking her from the back.

"Kamal! Please...put it in me, please!" Ondrea whined as she continued to cum multiple times in a row.

"Shhh," he commanded. "I'm not done taking care of you yet."

"OOOOH," she continued to cry out.

"Mm mm... you sound so good," Kamal moaned in response to knowing she was pleased with his foreplay technique. It was then that he decided to give it to her in the worst way. He flipped her back over on her back. "Kiss me, baby...it tastes like you...so sweet."

Ondrea kissed him passionately and was now a madwoman, pushing and trying everything that she could to press him into her wetness. He then retrieved his hardness from his underwear and entered her.

"Kamal!" she screamed in pleasure.

"Who?" he asked while he began playfully hitting every corner and crevice of the walls inside of her. He then thrust inside her with deep and intense strokes.

"Kamal!"

He then whispered in her ear, "Scream for me, lady..." then kissed her on the cheek.

Ondrea was done for and speechless as he began gliding in and out in a slow and steady motion. All she could do was cry tears when she released this time. He then proceeded to stroke in and out at a swift and fast pace until she could feel him throbbing inside of her. Then, warmth filled her up on the inside.

"AAAH!!!!" he grunted as he released inside his fiancée.

"Don't move. Just stay inside me, Kamal," Ondrea asked. He complied as they sealed their union with sensuous kisses until they fell asleep with their bodies still intertwined.

****

"Tyrin, don't stop!" Bria called out as she let her body release for a third time that night. He gave some more strokes before he followed suit and climaxed.

"I promise I need to bottle up what you got going on down there and keep it for myself...since I can't have all of you...it's the moves for me," Tyrin said as he leaned over to kiss her on lips.

"Shut up, 'Rin!" Bria responded as she got up, stumbling in soreness to the shower. She was still feeling the effects of the CBD Belle Body Royal gummies she and Tyrin had eaten before their encounter.

"Naw, but for real, though...what are we doing, Breeze?" Tyrin asked sincerely, laying back on her bed while admiring her body as she walked into her bathroom.

Bria felt wrong about meeting up with Tyrin today. 'D was preaching out of town at a conference; however, she had somehow convinced herself that he was only coming over to "talk."

"I don't know...I know we can't keep operating like this, though," I told you I'm happy..."

"—Yet you here laid up with me..."

"That's not fair, don't do that..."

"What you mean? You know I've been feeling you since high school...that ain't went nowhere."

"I know that, but I can't be with you, 'Rin. I made vows to God and my husband to stay committed—"

Tyrin laughed, "Committed?! You're going to the bathroom to wash up your little box after I have been all up in it, but you committed?"

"Glad you find this funny because I don't, Tyrin...matter of fact, you shouldn't even be here in the first place...get out...just, get out!"

"Are you serious?!"

"Yes!" Bria yelled at him as she ignored him and proceeded to get in the shower.

"Yeah, alright," Tyrin said as he got up and followed behind her...ready for round four.

Tyrin felt so good to her on so many levels. Dearron was her childhood sweetheart and husband who held his own in the bedroom and could cook also, but with him, there was always that constant pressure to be perfect. At times, he was overly critical of her. Bria had convinced herself that it was because of his position at his church where he pastored and in the local assembly that he held a position in. With Tyrin, she could let her "hair down," and there was always a no-judgment zone with him. Sometimes, she just needed that, and Tyrin had always been that for her.

*I was doing so good staying away from hooking up with him…* she thought as she looked at him, now passed out and snoring in his sleep. *I can stop after today, though, and it will be fine…* she rationalized in her head about her indiscretion. Bria thought about calling Ondrea and finally confessing to her to talk to her about it. Still, she knew that Ondrea did not want to speak to anyone for the past couple of days. She sighed…*I can't even go to Taylor about none of this now….Jesus, what have I done? Lord, I was doing so good…I'm not even going to come to you about this because, once again, I put myself in this situation. Help me shake loose from this man, in Jesus' name, Amen.*

Bria then dug into her old VHS collection. She popped in Juanita Bynum's famous message that helped her in her younger days—"No More Sheets."

# Chapter Seven-

It was 3:00 early in the morning when Tania was awakened by her cell phone ringing. She looked over...*Sebastian...now he knows he has some nerve trying to call me right now.*

"What?" Tania asked groggily, still trying to wake up to talk.

"Hey, babe—"

"Don't 'hey babe' me...why haven't you been answering my calls and leaving me on read?"

"Babe, my phone wasn't working, and I didn't know until after I finished talking to Reg... we are working on this science project together."

"Whatever, Sebastian...I don't believe you."

"Babe, I'm for real. Is your mom home? I can steal one of the cars and come see you..."

"Boy, you probably already did that, and right now she isn't, but I know you don't think you're coming over here when she can come home any time..."

"Where is all this coming from, babe? I don't understand because we were cool just earlier before practice..."

"Yeah, and that was before you stopped communication with me all day."

"The way you are coming at me, you sure you ain't got nobody you are dealing with?"

"While I'm giving all my energy and effort into us, that's when you don't have to worry. When I stop going off on you, then you have a reason to ask that question," Tania returned matter-of-factly.

"Yeah, alright," Sebastian retorted, "all I know is don't make me regret holding out if you on something else... I love you, and you should know by how many females I curve"—

"Oh, so you're saying you're doing me a favor?!"

"No, that's not what—"

"I got you, it's cool...you don't have to worry about holding out for the hoes anymore! I'm glad I never gave myself to you!"

*CLICK!*

Tania smiled to herself even while tears from anger started coming down her face. *Mom and Dad were right...thank You, Lord, I didn't fall with him like the devil wanted me to. My eyes are now open. Please forgive me for the sins I did commit with him...I won't be doing those anymore! I love You, Lord, and want to be pleasing in Your eyes like Dad says. Thank You, Lord, for deliverance.*

# Chapter Eight-

Kamal woke up at his usual time—4:30am. This

was his standard time for exercise routine—courtesy of Mr.

Sweatensity and sometimes Devan Allen of Pushing

Limits, followed by a meditation on God's Word. Instead,

he looked over at his wife-to-be sleeping so peacefully in

his bed, and for the first time in years, his routine was

thrown off. Realizing that they both were naked, Kamal

hurried to shower and get himself dressed before Ondrea

woke up. He had already felt guilty for going there with her

the way that he did last night. He wondered how she would

react upon awakening...*Lord, I pray I didn't scare her off.*

*I'm even more sorry for how I dropped the ball with You.*

Kamal's prayer was then cut short after hearing Ondrea

begin to stir in her sleep. *I know what I'll do,* Kamal

thought to himself as he grabbed a piece of paper and pen

to leave a note for her at the bedside while he snuck out to head down to the church.

*****

*Man, oh man, that was good!* Ondrea thought to herself as she opened her eyes, waking up. There was no better apology than the way that Kamal had put it down on her last night. *If this is what I have to look forward to in spending forever with him—then I have been rewarded for my pain and suffering,* she joked to herself. She rolled over to give him a kiss and realized that he was not there. She took notice; however, of a note in his place:

"Good morning, beautiful. I want to start off by saying last night, I was not prayed up as I should have been, and some things occurred between us that, while it felt good, should have never happened. I still hope you want to move forward with me as your husband and ask that if you would still have me, please meet me at the church. I'm already heading down there to repent first to my Lord and Savior. Secondly, waiting on you so that we can both be in unison on plans moving forward. Also, the towels are in the bathroom in a basket under the sink, and I also use Dove bar soap. I had to purchase some of that Cream Blends bath oil you had if you want to take one of those...you're welcome to whatever I have that you need. I have some fresh fruit on the kitchen counter and some croissants and sausage patties ready for you to heat up in the microwave. I love you, Ondrea Williams...hopefully Davis if your answer is still 'Yes.'"

Ondrea's heart smiled. She knew she wanted to spend the rest of her life with him. She quickly showered, got dressed, and ate the surprise breakfast he had prepared for her. Ondrea then made sure his bottom lock was locked to the front door as she hurried to meet him at the altar.

****

Bria had just finished her morning exercise routine with Peachy Fit, coupled with an early jog, and looked down at her Apple watch...6:00am. *Tyrin better be up and out of my house by the time I get back...* Just then, her phone began to ring.

"Talk to me!" she happily stated as she entered back into her home. Tyrin's Tesla had disappeared from her driveway, so she knew he was gone.

"Hey, girl!" Taylor exclaimed.

"Oh—H-hey...girl!" Bria stammered back. She didn't even take the time to screen the call beforehand. *Oh, Lord. I can't deal!*

"I know it's early, but I wanted to know if you'd pray with me for my morning prayer. I just feel like I've lost my way and really need to be in fellowship and conversation with sisters in Christ who are of strength to me."

"Taylor, I don't know if I'm the right person—I mean, you practically mentored me—"

"Which is why now, I need to reap the benefits of what's been poured into you. Bria, you're a First Lady, and right now, the only First Lady I know who is for real."

Immediately, Bria felt so guilty and remorseful of what she had done and to who she had betrayed. Taylor was the one who had been a friend first to her when everyone else had their backs turned and not receptive to Bria when Dearron got called to ministry. Taylor prayed with her all night, during the day when Bria first became the First Lady at her church. It was Taylor, who she vented to avoid mental and emotional breakdowns behind the rumors, lies, and drama from other women in 'D's congregation. Bria fought back the tears as she realized not only did she owe Taylor, but she had to make things right for her friend and sister in Christ.

"I got you, sis," Bria sighed. "Lord, Jesus Christ, I come to you humbly this morning in prayer and repentance. First, Lord, for not being perfect in Your sight... not being the woman of God that You called me to be. And secondly, in a prayer of thanks for giving me another chance and opportunity to get it right before You so that I can lift up clean and Holy hands. Lord, I ask that any sins committed knowingly and unknowingly by myself or my sister, that You forgive us. We thank and praise You for being the God that You are and for blessing us so far. We come to You also standing in need. I ask that whatever is troubling, ailing, discouraging, and frustrating my sister in You, that You deliver her so that she may have peace of mind and joy unspeakable. You said to cast our cares on You because

You care, so Lord, I pray that she has done just that as we close this prayer. In Jesus' name, we pray, Amen."

Taylor broke down crying over the phone, "Thank you so much, Bria! Thank You, Lord! Lord, please guide me on the right path...show me Your Will and Your Way. You know the thoughts and plans You have for me, and I know there's an expected end...God help me to hold on to Your unchanging hand. In Your name, Amen." Taylor then turned her attention to the incoming call she received from Tyrin. "Bria, I'll call you back later, Tyrin is beeping in, and he didn't come home last night—I have to see what's up with him."

"Sure, no problem," she said while trying not to show the remorse in her voice. *This MUST END, Lord, Jesus in Your name! Make it stop! Deliver me from Tyrin! I want my body to crave my husband only! I want my body to line up with your Word! The two shall be one flesh. I thank*

*You in advance that the marriage made in Heaven is now manifest here on Earth. It is so! Amen and Amen,* Bria declared with even more conviction. One thing Bria knew for sure is that God always answered her prayers.

****

"My apologies for taking so long. I had to make sure I changed clothes," Ondrea stated as she entered the sanctuary. She was cute and comfortable in an oversized sweatsuit with matching Nikes. Kamal was dressed coincidentally in a Nike tracksuit and matching shoes.

"No worries, lady," he replied. "I've used the extra time to just clear my head and get my mind right."

Ondrea chuckled. "Yeah, you were on another level last night, Minister."

"I know, Ondrea. That's partly why I invited you here with me in the first place. I wanted to apologize to

You before God in His tabernacle for disrespecting your body in the way that I did. Also, not to mention the inability to show temperance and allowing my anger to get the best of me. It turned into the complete loss of my emotions and ended up waking up next to you."

"Wait a minute, Kamal...I know I'm new to this whole no-sex-before-marriage thing—I mean, I didn't wait with Chance, but you're being too hard on yourself. You're human—"

"Yeah, I am, but do you know how many people use that as an excuse to do whatever it is that they want to do?"

*He has a good point.* Ondrea stayed silent and allowed him to continue.

"It is my job as a man of God to present you blameless before the Lord.... Ephesians 5:26..."

"I get that; I'm not knocking you for it either. I'm just saying that God is forgiving, and He won't hold it against you—"

"Should I continue in sin just because of His grace, though? God says, 'God forbid...' I can't allow myself to go there with you anymore until we are married."

"Then, let's speed up the process, Minister, because I want to connect with you again, and I think the good book says, 'It's better to marry than to burn—"

Kamal let out a hearty laugh, "Ondrea, you can't twist the scriptures to make them fit you," he teased. "You have to want to marry me, not just because we had sex, Ondrea."

"I know that. I'm just saying you already knew I wanted to marry you before that happened, Kamal."

"Lady, you are something else you know. As bad as I may want to rush things too…God's timing is everything. We still must make sure that we are planning for forever. We are going to need some counseling. I'd recommend both therapy and spiritual counseling. We need to make sure no cracks are left open for the enemy to come in, as you see already how he tried it. We're destined for greatness, Ondrea. But I'm afraid you also need to prepare yourself for what you're getting into with being married to a Pastor. Once I am elevated, you know there are new devils with these levels."

Ondrea looked up at Kamal with puppy-dog eyes, "I guess you're right...well, where do we begin?"

Kamal took her hand and led her up to the altar. "We start with repenting and making a vow right now before God that we will not allow what happened last night to happen again until Thanksgiving night—"

"And when that day comes, I sure will be thanking Him all night—"

"Stay focused, Ondrea." Kamal's tone became serious. *Lord, I am strong in You.* "I need you to help me to stay strong, lady. With you, I'm someone else, and it's the carefree Kamal, without all the negativity, of course...but, to simply put it—I can't go there with you. I need you to understand that. It's the ministry first until we are married—more importantly, God first, babe."

She realized the sincerity and pleading in his voice concerning the anointing that he did not want God to strip from him if he stayed disobedient to his Word. Furthermore, Ondrea did not want to be a hindrance to her husband-to-be.

"You're right, babe. I will make sure that I stay strong for you and help you not to fall...even if it means wearing baggy clothes in your presence—"

"Ondrea, you could have on anything, and I'm turned on...it's all of you for me, and that's the problem...well, for right now, anyway," he chuckled again.

"Kamal, all jokes aside, I'm willing to help in any way that I can. You also can't show any of your muscles around me. I definitely can't see those tattoos anymore until we're married either...which means no swimming together until after the wedding..."

"Hold up, what do you mean? Summer is coming up ..."

"It's the tattoos and all of your fineness for me," she replied playfully. "I cannot see the tattoos because they do something to me," she admitted.

"Do you even know what they are and what they represent? I got them when I was first saved and didn't know any better about marking up my body. The cross on my back with Philippians 3:13 &14 represents Christ dying on the cross for me and that all my sins that I committed in my former life are now forgiven. I press on forward in Jesus Christ...it was my 'road to redemption' tattoo....the one on my chest just had Jeremiah 29:11...reminding me that I don't know all of the plans God has for me, but I know He's given me an expected end that if I remain in Him, I will be victorious over whatever and whoever comes my way."

"You can't stop preaching, even if you wanted to," Ondrea said in awe of what Kamal had previously stated over his life. "I feel so honored to be connected with you, Kamal. You have shown me so many things and opened my mind up to so many thoughts about God that I have never had before—let alone experienced since I gave my life to Him."

"You never know what you can go through or deal with when you're in Him. Always remember, Ondrea, that it's not by might or power of our own, but by His Spirit that we can carry on."

"Amen …. Amen!"

The two of them prayed together at the altar. Afterward, Ondrea left to go to work and finished up her evening, spending some time with Tania. At the same time, Kamal eagerly called his best friend to share the good news.

**** 

"What's good, my brother?" Dearron asked as he pulled in at the nearest gas station to gas up and drive back home from the convention. He had been praying fervently, asking for favor and grace to be applied to his friend and brother in the gospel, Kamal. After the revelation hit about him being responsible for Chance's murder, Dearron knew that he had favor with God. He could ask Him a hard thing…this was a hard thing. He made sure that he fasted every day for three days. He also made sure that he prayed every day at 7:00pm. He believed for God to do a complete work in Ondrea and Kamal's relationship—he loved them and the couples fellowship they had together that much.

"I can't call it, brother…how was the convention?"

"Well, let's just say Jonoah's college fund will have a nice amount added."

"God is good. I thank God for your mentorship and friendship, brother. I can only pray that I can be as much of a blessing to Ondrea and Tania as you are with your family."

"Brother, you two will have another baby—watch and see. I see the way that you look at each other, and wedding night, we know it's going down—"

"That's what I wanted to talk to you about..."

"What?" Dearron asked, growing concerned.

Kamal sighed, "...man, I slipped up with her last night—"

"Hold up...brother, are you telling me what I think you're telling me?"

"Yeah—"

"That's great—I mean, oh wow..."

Kamal chuckled, "I know what you mean."

"So, it's safe to say that we aren't speaking in faith

anymore and that the wedding is still on?"

"That's the move."

"Alright now, brother…that's what we wanna hear—I mean, the wedding part. You better keep it in your pants, though, doc. If you want to make sure God honors what ya'll are trying to do…some days, I wonder if Bria and I having sex before marriage on the regular made it a curse."

"What are you saying? You know you weren't saved then, right?"

"True, but there are still consequences to sin that no one is exempt from…you should know…"

"Touché," Kamal responded.

"So, now you see where the concern is."

Dearron never had a reason to feel insecure until he saw the way his wife had looked at Taylor when she got up to run after Tyrin during Kamal and Ondrea's engagement party. Up until then, 'D knew that his wife was pleased sexually and spiritually by him, emotionally though—he wondered if she was all the way present with him at times. The fact that in high school, she cheated on his twin brother, Dane, for him all started to come back together. *'D, you tripping man… it's just the enemy trying to make you see things that aren't there…but God also gives us discernment? God, I need to hear YOUR voice, loud and clear. I don't understand, but I'm picking up a vibe between my wife and another man. Please show me what that is, Lord. I want peace of mind over this situation and in my home. In Jesus's name!*

"'D, I really don't think it's nothing, man…Bria

loves you—that I know anyone can discern. Remember, they both were in "the life" …they probably have seen and witnessed some things go down that they can't share. Trust me, I know how the game goes."

"You know what? Thanks, brother…you're probably right…I'm glad I have somebody I can trust to bounce off my thoughts and get some godly counsel."

"Anytime, man. I thank you for helping me go to war to get my lady back."

"Sure thing, brother. Just next time something like this happens, don't go using your spear until November. You know the best warriors even put their spears down on Sundays," Dearron said jokingly.

"Aye, man…you're wilding for that one!" Kamal returned laughing, "But I hear you, brother…and trust me, that is duly noted."

# Chapter Nine-

BRRIIIING!!!!

Tania wanted to avoid Sebastian as much as possible today. Low and behold, he was waiting for her at her locker.

"Morning, Tania," he stated as she approached to retrieve her books. She looked extra beautiful with her hair down in curls, wearing some Ugg moccasins, black Pop Fit tights, and a tan cardigan sweater.

"What are you doing here? I thought I told you that you don't have to worry about holding out on other females anymore. I'm good."

"Calm down, babe, I didn't mean it that way…"

"No... you meant it just the way you put it. You were mad that I didn't want you to come over so you can try again to get some...I mean it, I'm good."

Sebastian stood there in shock. He never even saw this coming where Tania would switch up positions on him. He just knew that eventually, she would give in—not give up!

"Tania, I love you—"

"I'm gonna stop you right there, Sebastian. Love is patient and doesn't pressure someone into having sex. If I told you once that that's not something I wanted to do, then you should have respected me enough not to keep trying it. Secondly, I don't think that I will ever be ready to give my virginity to anyone other than my husband. If you already are having trouble dealing with that, then I'm not the one for you."

"Oooh," said a crowd that was now gathering around her locker. Tania didn't realize how loud she was.

"If she doesn't give it to you, you know I'm down, boo...I've been feeling you," said Seneca. She was the beautiful, Hispanic, and popular junior who just so happened to be one of his classmates in AP English.

Tania glared at Seneca, "You can have him...I'm done dealing with these problems." Tania slammed her locker shut and ran down the hallway and out into the parking lot. It was only the beginning of the 1st period... *I'm outta here!* She then got into her car with tears running down her face and sped off to Lenox Mall to do some retail therapy at her favorite store—Forever 21.

****

Tania had just left out of Forever 21. She headed over to the Tory Burch store to window shop when she felt someone come up behind her, covering her eyes. She smelled the Bourbon scent from Bath & Bath Body Works' male collection.

"How are you doing, Reginae—I mean, Ms. Tania?" he said while licking his lips in approval. She was stunningly gorgeous to him, and he loved the effort she put into always looking a perfect ten whenever she stepped out.

"Boy, you need to stop," she returned with a slight chuckle, "what are you doing out here?"

"I should be asking you the same question…aren't you supposed to be in class, young lady?" he said with a wink.

"Boy—stop! You are petty!" she exclaimed, playfully hitting him in the arm.

"So, I'm gonna be forward with you if that's alright, Miss 'T…"

Tania crossed her arms in a defensive stance and braced herself for Sincere's question.

"It's not even like that. I just wanted to ask if you're seeing someone. I know it's not a secret that I've been feeling you for a while—I mean, I hope you could tell…my grandma would approve of you for sure."

"But you know of me, Sincere…you don't really know me though—"

"What do you think I'm trying to ask you, 'T?"

"Then, I'd say that if you're trying to get to know me, you would know that 'T is my cousin Tyrin's nickname—"

"Okay, okay, so you'll be my 'Sweet T.'"

She blushed at the nickname he had already started to call her...*He is sooo fine...and looks so good in his Balmain fit*, "that's corny...but cute."

Sincere grinned ear-to-ear in response to Tania's acceptance of the pet name he made up for her. "So this means you're all mine?"

"I belong to Jesus Christ, homie...unless you're trying to put a ring on it, sir, that's it, and that's all."

"That's fair...we'll have to do something about that, now, don't we?"

"What do you mean?"

"Do you believe in love at first sight?"

Tania was overwhelmed at his question and even more confused at why she wasn't bothered by it either.

"To be honest, I've never thought about that before, Sincere."

"Well, with me, I'm about to turn you on to some new stuff…I can promise you that."

"Should I be scared to be with you?" she asked nervously.

Tania was already rebounding from Sebastian, but at the same time, she wanted to experience being the girlfriend of THE Sincere Phillips. He could choose to go pro in basketball or be a successful engineer was so sexy to her, and the ultimate come up. *Sebastian won't even know what to do with himself when he sees who I pulled. Forget him! I'm so glad I didn't give him my virginity. Okay— focus on Mr. Fine right now, sis. He is so sexy. Lord, help!*

"You don't have to be scared of me...I'll only take you where you're ready to go—for sure...trust me, I'm way too busy with basketball and school to try and complicate your life. I just know that when I first saw you, I knew that I needed you in mine."

"Awww, what makes you believe that?"

"Because you have an aura about you that represents strength, but an overwhelming vulnerability...I want to nurture that on top of knowing that you are the 'loyal' type—"

"—And you? Are you loyal?"

"Most definitely. I saw my father and mother both cheat on each other while growing up. That's something that I promised myself that whoever I'm with won't have to worry about that from me...plus, you are so bad, Sweet

'T…I don't know how anyone could play around on you."

"You'd be surprised."

"Well, we are gonna concentrate on just us from this moment on, love."

"I like that idea," Tania replied and reached out to hug him.

As soon as they hugged, Sincere's phone began to ring. They both looked at each other as if they already knew what the phone call was for. Tania grabbed him again—this time tighter, and he squeezed her back, thankful in that moment for the comfort.

# Chapter Ten-

"She's gone, but it's to a better place," Minister Kamal began to give the eulogy during Mother Helen's funeral service. "Matthew 5:16 says for us to let our light so shine so that men can see our good works, and therefore God will get the glory…Mother Helen did just that—she let her Soul Glow, baby!"

Everyone in the congregation chuckled at Minister Kamal's reference to Coming To America. Mother Helen was a solid fan. She always joked that she wanted her funeral centered around the movie—down to her brother's friend Jeffrey singing the famous theme song from the Soul Glo commercial. The fact that the family had to push her funeral back another week so he could be there to sing was how serious they took her request.

"This is how we will remember her—silly, full of life, spirit, and joy. Mother Helen was saved. So although we will miss her presence here on Earth, we will be comforted to know that she accepted our Lord and Jesus Christ as her personal Savior. She did not deviate from The Word, and for us to see her again on the other side, then we are going to have to make sure that we are doing what is asked of us in His kingdom  to make Heaven our home."

"You're talking right, Minister," said one of the Deacons in the congregation.

"So, for some of you right now...I hear you asking me, 'Minister, how do I know if I'm doing what I'm supposed to do to make Heaven my home? Well, for starters, judge yourself from the Word so that you don't have to worry about being judged later. Holding the Word up to you like a mirrored reflection is the best self-assessment you can administer. One of the best scriptures you can use to make sure you're on the right track is Galatians 5:22… Now, verses 16-21 of the same chapter go into everything that you better not do, but we wanna focus on the things we're supposed to have. The fruit that our tree is supposed to produce is love, joy, peace, long-suffering, gentleness, goodness, faith, meekness, and temperance. All of these are rooted in the essence of God—which is love. For He loved us so much that in John 3:16 it says, He gave His only begotten Son."

"Thank You, Jesus," Sincere's mother shouted.

"When we don't produce the fruit that Christ is looking for upon his return, guess what will happen? Mark 11: 12-25 speaks to when Jesus found a fig tree not producing any fruit, He then cursed it, and it died…People, this is how we die emotionally—which turns into spiritual death—that ultimately leads us into a life of sin, and physical death. We're cursed or damned to Hell when we live a lifestyle that's contrary to God's Word. Saints and friends of God, if we want to make Heaven our home, then we have to show love—not the fake, conditional stuff either—but that Christ kind of love...that deep love."

Minister Kamal then looked over at Ondrea, who in turn looked back at him and smiled. *"Lord, thank You for giving me a forgiving spirit," she prayed silently to herself. "Thank You for refreshing me and Kamal's connection with each other. I thank You that you allowed us the opportunity to continue building on the foundation that we had started to build as friends and confidantes."*

"We can't cut people off and out of our lives because you never know when or if God just might use that person to be of encouragement, or even the vessel for your blessing down the line. Our ways are not His ways...We need to have that joy...remember the joy of the Lord is our strength. Peace of mind is also in Him. Long-suffering is tied with patience. What amazes me is how we are willing to cut others off…all while God still wakes our crusty behinds up every morning. He allows us way past the seventy times seven chances to get ourselves together…*but God doesn't know what he's doing…how dare someone else to cross us, and we have to forgive them as if it never happened*, is what we think…but we want God to do the same for us?"

"Ouch!" a member expressed.

"Yes, if you can't say Amen, say 'ouch…' we all have work to do. Gentleness and goodness are self-explanatory…faith—He said it's impossible to please him without it. We must first believe that He is, and if He is, then there's no room for doubt. Meekness is being able to take low sometimes—not be a punk, but having humility and temperance—or self-control… Again, Saints—we got this! We can do this as long as we remain alive in Him and work towards perfection to produce the fruit God is looking for in this Garden of Life. If there's anyone here who does not know Jesus Christ in the pardon of their sins...if interested in starting your journey in letting God pluck out the weeds of your life to help you produce the fruit that won't curse your life, please come forward."

Immediately, five people came up to give their lives to Christ—including Sincere. All five of them received the gift of the Holy Spirit also. Tania was pleasantly surprised. *I never saw*

*a boy my age wanting to really serve God...he's crying too? Wow, God, you are showing me some things for real. I've been missing out on this saved boyfriend stuff. Thanks, Mother Helen, for your life and in it, allowing me to meet Sincere.*

\*\*\*\*

"What about Mr. Sincere is going on that you gotta be smiling about?" Londyn noticed and asked Tania as she waddled up to her to hug her after the funeral. Her stomach had really gotten bigger.

Tania's smile began to get wider by the minute.

"Oooh, you're cheesing hard, too!" Londyn exclaimed. "Are you two 'a thing' now?"

"I don't know what you're talking about…"

"In my Rude Boys voice as the song says, 'It's written all over your face,'" she said as she taunted Tania while singing the words. "Okay, so you're modest now...heffa, just say you guys are together so ish can be confirmed...I already know about you and Sebastian's break-up, I mean everybody and they mama knows—"

"I don't wanna discuss that piece of sh—"

"Girl, we are still in God's house!" Londyn could tell she had hit a nerve with Tania and was not going to let her try to deflect or distract any attention from the subject at hand.

"You're right...Lord, please forgive me for my anger and frustration with all of my situations...in Jesus' name, I pray, Amen," Tania quickly prayed aloud after realizing her triggered anger with Sebastian.

"Amen and Amen, sis."

Just then, Tania and Londyn saw Sincere heading their way. "The moment of truth has arrived!" said Londyn with a smile.

"Girl, you better not…" Tania said while trying to cover Londyn's mouth.

"Good afternoon, ladies," said Sincere as he gave both of them hugs.

"And so we meet after a service again," teased Londyn.

"Indeed," he replied. He quickly shot a wink at Tania, "Thanks so much for coming out to celebrate my grandmother's life...both of you." Sincere turned his head back to Tania, "Sweet T, you are such a refresher when life has been rough for me lately...thank you."

Both he and Tania locked eyes with each other and smiled. Londyn felt like the uncomfortable third wheel and bowed out of their conversation gracefully.

"Ummm hmmm...alrighty then, I'm gonna just leave you two be...I knew y'all were 'a thing'," she said as she gave Sincere a hug goodbye and began to head back over to her parents.

Sincere laughed, "I take it that she found out about us being a couple now?"

"Yep, that would be correct...so, how are you holding up?"

"I'm telling you if it wasn't for you and God, I would be trashed right now."

"What does that mean?" Tania asked.

"High and drunk…"

"You mean like alcohol and weed?"

"All of that, babe...I even used to pop pills, too...that's why I'm so glad that I made the decision to give my life to Christ at one of our campus revivals. I knew I needed to live a better way, but college life will get to you when and if you're not prepared for it as you think... man, I have seen and done too much out there..."

"Wow, you better thank Jesus for the deliverance, homie...I don't see you any different at all. My dad says to never judge a person by what they do because man will look for the obvious [signs]. However, God sees their hearts and whether or not that person could be crying out to Him in the middle of their sin for Him to help then to overcome whatever it is that has a hold on them."

"That's good stuff...when I was getting high, I wasn't asking for God to save me—let alone help me to stop what I was doing...sin feels good. Don't let anyone lie and tell you that it doesn't."

"Dang, you are really delivered then, huh? I mean, I can't even tell that you were the type of person that wanted or needed to get high and drunk."

"Yeah, I still crave alcohol—especially when I'm at the parties on campus, but other than that, I am one hundred percent delivered."

"So, what do you do when the cravings are too much? I thank God that substances were never my struggle or issue."

"You better thank God that monkey didn't jump on your back. No, but for real, when it comes to cravings, that's when I have to be honest with myself and not go to the parties they may be having, or when the alcohol gets flowing, that's my cue to exit."

At that moment, Sincere's life flashed right before him. He would forever be grateful to the Lord for delivering him and setting him back on the right path. The journey in his freedom to become a man of God that everyone could smile was something for him to be proud of. That he made it through.

"That's awesome that you do not deceive yourself and that you have that sense of self-awareness," Tania said with excitement. She cherished the maturity of Sincere. She learned something new with every encounter she had with him. Something different from Sebastian.

****

"Yeah, heffa, you ain't slick!" Londyn told Tania later over their Facetime.

"Whatever," she retorted.

"And what's up with the 'Sweet T' thing, huh? Sincere already has pet names for you? Are you sure you guys haven't been keeping your relationship under wraps for longer than what I know?"

"No, no...I promise it's not even like that, sissy...as far as the nickname, it's actually the type of corny I like— not to mention that it's super cute."

"Yeah, yeah...OUCH!" Londyn shouted out loud.

A growing concerned look spread across Tania's face, "What's wrong?"

"Nothing," she lied. The baby was starting to kick a little more forceful now, and sometimes she was not ready for when the kicks occurred.

"Yea, okay..."

"Why are you trying to change the subject?" asked Tania.

"I figured you felt there was too much discussion regarding your new boo."

"What's going on with you and my cousin?"

"Actually, your cousin and I are doing just fine...he's been so patient with me the entire time. He's always asking if I need anything, and 'T keeps those back massages as well as that 'D' on the regular!"

"Really? Now, this is some news worth celebrating—minus the 'D' part," Tania stated while laughing. "You know that's how ya'll got in this situation now...ya'll better get married before ya'll make any more nieces and nephews!"

"I know, right? Your cousin is off the chain trying to sneak out of the house so he can go and get my cravings late at night. I think that my parents may be suspecting something is up because my mother kept asking me about my period. My father has been looking at T all weird whenever he comes over to chill with me during the day and on the weekends...I know something is up."

"Well, don't feel too bad. I mean, eventually, your parents are gonna have to find out anyway. You guys better tell them before school is out for sure...that way, this summer, you should be off of punishment by then. You and I can tear up these streets in our cars and still do some harmless flirting with hot guys while enjoying our boyfriends."

"You are a hot mess, sis...I'm doing good to hold onto T. I hate that I can't have a 'hot girl' summer, though...I really wanted to be able to stunt on these heauxs for sure..."

"You still can, Londy," Tania insisted. "Shein, ASOS, and Old Navy have some cute maternity clothes. Let's hit some stores up now if you're not too tired for some, and that can also be motivation for you guys to go ahead and spill the beans."

"I guess, sis...let me tell my parents I'm gonna ride with you."

"Alright, and I'll let my parents know, and check in with Sincere to see if he and T wanna meet up with us wherever we stop for some pizza or something."

"I want South City Kitchen Midtown," Londyn added.

"There are those cravings...I bet you want some of their biscuits or cornbread?"

"You know it!" Londyn laughed. "The other day, I ordered some of Premium by the Pound's Brown Sugar Pound Cake through Goldbelly....girl, I am on pins and needles waiting to taste the delicious flavor!"

"Now that's what I'm jealous about...you can eat whatever you want right now and blame it on the baby."

"I guess you're right, sis."

"Well, I'll call and tell Sincere..."

"And I'll just text T...see you in twenty?"

"Sure," Tania said as they hung up, and she prepared to leave.

# Chapter Eleven-

During March and April, Bria and Dearron
continued their lives together in harmony. Dearron noticed
Bria being more loving and attentive to him after Ondrea
and Kamal reconciled. He definitely had no complaints;
however, he still could not shake the feeling that something
was up. Bria was godly sorry for her affair. She repented of
her sins and had since turned away from Tyrin—who had
finally stopped trying to reach back out to Bria towards the
end of April.

Tyrin realized that Bria would not leave Dearron for
him, decided to accept the harsh reality, and get back to
focusing on expanding his brand with his construction
company and auto bodywork, getting his bag. Somehow, in
the back of his mind, he said that he would be ready

whenever the day came that Bria decided that she wanted to be with him again.

Tyrin and Taylor continued their fling until he felt that Taylor had overstepped her boundaries when she became privy to information that he was going to be a grandfather around August. Taylor had told him that it wasn't that bad of a mistake and to stop hitting 'T while he was in a raging fit after Tyrin Jr. confessed to the rumor. Tyrin knew that it was more than just a mistake, but a game-changer that had life-long lasting effects. It was not long after that incident when Taylor realized that at that point, Tyrin solely was with her for sex and not companionship. She wanted more and eventually started to move on with a prominent investment banker.

On the other hand, Londyn's parents were surprisingly more supportive than Tyrin. While they still were highly disappointed in their only child's decision to have unprotected sex and become pregnant, the fact that her boyfriend was a very bright young man helped them to not write 'T completely off. Londyn's mother joked with her all the time about

not staring into his "baby blues." All they asked for was that 'T be supportive for Londyn and their baby girl, Journey. That will be her name, as it symbolizes the "journey" that they all are in for whenever she arrives.

Kamal and Ondrea made significant gains and progress in their weekly marital counseling. They received counseling from both Kamal's spiritual covering and couple's counseling from the world-renown Jim and

Elizabeth Carroll from Marriage Boot Camp. They began to identify possible triggers that could arise and prove to be detrimental to their upcoming marriage. They started the process of dealing with their own personal traumas from childhood: abandonment and grief & loss.

They still could not find resolve on the issue of whether or not to tell Tania the ugly truth. Kamal said that he felt anything that's done in the dark always comes to light. While agreeing to this theory, Ondrea also knew her daughter and thought they should protect her from feeling even more pain. She explained to Kamal that emotionally it's already tough on Tania not having her father, but this would ultimately crush her.

****

Tania and Sincere started to become closer to each other since he could not go back to school until after her mom's birthday. There were so many layers to Tania, and

Sincere wanted to help her unravel them. He wasn't perfect, but he was a young man who was trying to be something for himself and his family—all while making God proud of him. He had envisioned making her his wife a lot of the time, but he didn't want to scare her off. *In due time...*

Tania couldn't believe how Sincere instantly clicked with both Londyn and 'T. She thought that 'T was probably happier to hang out with Sincere out of everyone considering that he was goal status in the career/sports path. Date nights on the weekends were a joy whenever Londyn was not feeling tired. Tania also couldn't help but feel happy that Sebastian was devastated after learning that she had moved on—better yet, with who she moved on with.

Tania was also impressed with the way that she was being spoiled by Sincere. From hair and nail salon trips, love notes that were hidden in her purse or car, to him giving her all the kisses and hugs that she craved…She had already let Sincere know that he couldn't count on getting any from her. Still, he was alright with it—never brought the subject up to her… *nothing*…no grabbing her butt or copping extra feels?…*Maybe he does love me?*

# Chapter Twelve-

"Good morning, cow," Ondrea said to Bria with a warm embrace and sat back down. They had met up at Chef Vino's restaurant for their standing monthly Saturday brunch with shopping afterward.

"Morning, cow," Bria replied with not as much enthusiasm as Ondrea while hugging her back. She was not feeling too well but could not even think of standing up her BFF of ten plus years with a no-show.

"Are you alright?" Ondrea asked with a puzzled look on her face. She could tell something was up with her best friend.

"Yeah, girl…it's just my stomach has been acting funny lately. I hope it's not anything serious."

Ondrea eyed Bria cautiously, "Then you didn't have to travel all this way, and you feel like crap...we could have just re-scheduled—"

Bria rushed to get up from her chair and darted to the restroom. Ondrea got up to follow behind her to make sure that her friend was okay.

"Bria!" she called out as she searched for the correct bathroom stall.

"Over here," she confirmed.

"Cow, are you alright?!" Ondrea stated with concern.

It was then that Bria had no choice but to confess and confide the inevitable to Ondrea. "I am starting to think that I might be pregnant...I have a test right here in my purse."

"I knew it had to be something like this...well, come on and take it!"

After cleaning up from vomiting, Bria then retrieved the pregnancy test from her purse and proceeded to pee on the stick. Two lines.

"Congrats... I'm going to be an auntie again!" Ondrea exclaimed. There was silence from Bria, and at that moment, Ondrea knew there was more to this story. "Okay, so what's the matter with being pregnant? 'Noah is going to need a playmate anyway...what is 'D saying about all of this?—"

"No!" Bria shouted, forgetting that she was in a public restroom.

"Girl, what is the matter?! Come on, let's go to my car for a second," Ondrea suggested.

After the two got inside Ondrea's SUV, Bria felt free to let the tears flow freely down her face. "I don't want to let 'D know anything yet."

"Why? You know he'll be happy—"

"I don't know if I even want to keep this one—"

"Hold up...I know you're not thinking about doing something stupid...you already know how hard it was for you two to conceive, Jonoah...what's really going on?"

Bria took a long pause before beginning to explain. "So, there may be a chance that this baby isn't Dearron's." She searched Ondrea's face for a response; however, she stared back at her with an emotionless gaze.

"How is this even possible? You've been holding out on me for real...who else have you been with, Bria?"

" 'Rin—Tyrin—"

Ondrea covered her mouth in shock, "No way! How long has this been going on?!" She had suspicions that they had messed around while in high school, but never did she picture them hooking up recently. Then again, she began to flashback. Not only did she remember Bria's reaction when Ondrea told her that she would tell Tyrin hello after she divulged that Tyrin was out of prison, but also during Ondrea and Kamal's engagement party. Ondrea remembered when she had observed how Bria reacted when Tyrin and Taylor had shown up together. The signs were there all along.

"Off and on since I was sixteen…I hadn't had sex with him in years. I did not start messing back with him until around your engagement party weekend. Since then, and even more so after talking to Taylor recently, I haven't hooked up with him anymore."

"Oh my goodness, cow! What did Taylor say?!"

"We didn't talk about that. Taylor had actually called me and asked me to pray for her because she felt like she had lost her way and ironically wanted to gain some strength from me! It was almost as if God used her to get me to stop. I couldn't keep betraying 'D or Taylor in so many respects…they both don't deserve that—no one does."

"Do you think you love him?"

"No," Bria rushed in. "I know my heart always will belong with Dearron…he's so good to me and good for me, but with 'Rin, you know when I was out there being trafficked, he rescued me—"

"—So your feelings for him are described almost similar to the Nightingale Effect."

"What's that?" Bria inquired.

"It's when caregivers fall in love with their patients—derived from the nurse Florence Nightingale because she showed so much care and compassion towards everyone that was in her care. Maybe that's the bond you two developed—he cares deeply for you and you the same because of what he did for you."

"Maybe you're right, 'Drea," Bria agreed. "I just know if I decide to have this baby and it comes out with baby blues like little 'T, then there's gonna be some smoke in the city."

Ondrea nodded in agreement, "Yeah, your hubby does not play about you, and to know what happened—"

"Okay, you don't have to remind me, cow," Bria chimed in. "Now, can you see why it isn't worth that risk?"

"As scary as it sounds and maybe... I still can't see risking an innocent baby's life...I mean, what if it's the girl you guys have always wanted? It would be an even boy and girl..."

"I appreciate the encouragement, sister, but I just can't get with that rationale."

"I hear you, cow...but please promise me you'll pray on that before you make any decisions."

"Okay, I promise," Bria agreed and locked pinkies with Ondrea in a pinky promise. "So," she added while changing the subject, "do you have any revelations, miss-missy?"

Ondrea forgot that Kamal's boy was her bestie's husband and that he probably shared the news with him. "What are you referring to?"

"How about you and Kamal?"

Ondrea sighed, "yeah, we have been attending marriage counseling the past couple of months, and since the slip up we had right before Mother Helen's passing, we haven't been intimate since—"

"Hold up!" Bria shifted in the passenger seat. "You two did it?"

Ondrea was hoping that she didn't have to relive the night of pure bliss that she still craved so bad and secretly prayed for like it was devotion. She clutched her pearls around her neck, "Girl…that's not even the words to describe—"

"I told you, 'Drea…I could tell the Minister was a monster in those sheets…he's so serious in his demeanor, so you know he doesn't play when it comes to the matters in the bedroom."

"Yeah, but the messed up part about it is that not only can we not do it again before we get married, but he also came in me."

"Shut up! So, how far back are we talking?"

"Like the end of February…"

"That's around the same time for me too, sis…do you think you could be pregnant?"

"I don't think so…I'm still getting my cycle and no nausea like I had with Tania."

"Yeah, but you were eighteen then, 'Drea…our bodies have changed since then."

"I guess you're right."

"Well, promise you'll let me know if you need to take a test—wait, so what do you do when it gets to calling you?"

"You mean the cravings?"

"Yes, heffa...Chances, cousin? Come on now, you know, I know," Bria said, laughing.

"Well, I just use my rose to take the edge off. I find myself using it every time before I meet up with him somewhere. I even use it before it's time for our nightly conversations, so I'm not tempted to start up something with him."

"Temperance, honey...that's a mean thing. Especially when you guys are only five months away from the wedding...What about him?"

"Girl, he stays prayed up so that he's always in the right headspace...me, not as much. I need deliverance from my husband-to-be's penis! Well, not total deliverance, just up until the wedding," Ondrea laughed, "so moving forward, if I call you for a scripture or prayer before meeting up with that man, now you know why."

"Gotcha…and I will do the same. Whenever 'Rin's thang gets to calling me again, I will make sure I call you first for scripture or prayer. He hasn't contacted me recently, but bay-bee, he puts it down, so I will make sure to have you on standby."

"First of all, TMI," Tania added jokingly. "Thank God for friendship—and true

friendship at that…we will hold each other accountable as the women of God that He has purposed for us to be!" Ondrea stated.

"Amen, cow…Amen."

The two then exited the SUV and went back inside

the restaurant to finish ordering their food so that they could continue their day as planned.

****

"Do you want me to push up the wedding date, babe? You know we can't beat Tania and Sincere to the altar," asked Kamal jokingly. It was now seven o'clock, and he and Ondrea were at the church for marriage counseling. They had just finished hugging each other and now staring at each other with dreamy eyes. "I'm trying to stay as strong as I can."

"Temptation is a mutha, and I don't think that Tania will say 'yes' just yet…that's the only reason I went along with his request. I'm surprised you agreed that he could, also."

"A man knows when he knows, babe," Kamal replied. "Besides, I agree that she will believe it's too soon as well...they'll be alright...now back to us, though..."

Ondrea added. "We've been doing good so far. Let's continue following your direction. What did our counselor just get finished telling us? He said we need to make sure we iron out everything that we can think of before then."

"Okay, love...I want to kiss you, but my spiritual father said that kissing gets you pregnant..."

Ondrea let out a hearty laugh, "Boy, stop!"

"I'm serious," he responded back playfully.

"The last time we kissed, I could have gotten pregnant, you know—"

"Don't remind me, lady…that's why we need to move the date up."

"So, you think I'm pregnant—please don't tell me God showed you that…"

"No, He didn't show me that. I have a feeling, though, that if you aren't now, by the time we come back from our honeymoon, you will be."

"I want us to be able to enjoy each other as husband and wife first, though, Kamal."

"I know, lady. I'll try my best to be on my best behavior."

"I'll just try the pill again. I wasn't very successful the first time around that I tried—"

"Alright, I don't want to hear about you with anyone else sexually."

"Yes, sir," Ondrea replied with a smirk. She knew not to call him "daddy," or it would be over for the both of them, and they'd be right back in sin.

"I appreciate you are trying to help me to stay strong spiritually, 'Drea…" he knew the sacrifices she was making in place of them being intimate with each other and the restraint in

trying to tempt him with her words, "…another reason I need you to be my wife."

"I got you, babe…for life," Ondrea responded with a wink.

"That's what's up," Kamal replied as they walked outside. He escorted Ondrea up to her car door and opened it. "Remember to make sure you let me know when you make it home safely."

They both agreed to keep their phone calls to a minimum due to talking long. They started "talking wrong." Five months was not moving by as fast as they would have wanted it to be. At the same time, they knew that they had to play everything according to God's plan if they wanted Him to smile on their union. They wanted God to heal the wounds internally, individually, and corporately between the two of them.

# Chapter Thirteen-

"So, after this birthday dinner for your mom, you trying to hang with me for a little. You know I have to have you fly to Philly for a bit?" Sincere asked Tania.

With only one more week away from heading back to school, he wanted to propose to Tania, but he wasn't sure how well she would take it. He had already asked both Ondrea and Minister Kamal, and to his surprise, they gave their blessings. He had requested Londyn to come with him to pick out Tania's ring. Still, with Londyn now seven months pregnant—and miserable—she opted for a FaceTime meet-up instead. They settled for a 2-carat princess-cut diamond ring from Zales.

"You know I want to spend as much time with you as I can before you go back, bae. These past few months with you have been nothing short of amazing," Tania stated. She wanted to make sure that she let Sincere know how much she had enjoyed her boyfriend and equally the time spent together.

"I agree, Sweet T," Sincere stated. "I wish we didn't have to have all this space between us when I head back to school…" he said, hugging her, and then began daydreaming about what that special moment will be like when he popped the question.

"Me either…how soon can I come to visit you when you go back?"

"I don't know, babe…"

Tania suddenly became alarmed, "What do you mean? What's wrong with me coming to see you?"

Sincere held both Tania's hands and said with a firm tone, "It's not you...it's definitely me...I mean, I don't trust myself alone with you staying the night in my dorm room—in my bed—"

"Relax, homie! Who said I was going to stay in your dorm or, better yet, in your bed with you?"

"Yeah, okay...so where were you gonna sleep then?"

"In your bed...alone, though."

"So, where does that leave me?"

"On the floor by me," she said matter-of-factly.

"On my granny, that's not even about to go down like that..." he said slyly and playfully began tickling her.

"Oh yes, it will!" Tania shrieked while trying to run and escape being tickled.

# Chapter Fourteen-

"What you mean they're getting married?!" Tyrin demanded.

"Pop, Tania was all happy today after school, telling us about cousin Ondrea and Minister Kamal working things out. They have been going to counseling and still going to get married."

"So, she knows about what happened?" asked Tyrin, confused.

"What happened?"

At that moment, he knew that Tania still had no clue as to who Minister Kamal really was or what "Ice" did to her father. "Nevermind, son…I'll be back."

"Who, Dad?" 'T was confused as to what was going on. His father had stormed out of the house in a rage and sped off in his Tesla.

He then picked up the phone to text and alerted Tania, **"Hey cuz…I don't know what's going on, but Dad is mad and on his way over to y'all house."**

**"Thanks, cuz…I'll listen out for him."**

\*\*\*\*

Tyrin rang the doorbell five times back to back while Ondrea got up out of her bed to answer the door. "Hey, cuz—"

"Don't 'hey cuz' me…you still messing with that nigga?"

" 'Rin, what are you talking about? Don't you know it is almost midnight?"

"Man, you can miss me with all that…you really about to still marry this nigga?"

"Don't even come at me with anything dealing with marriage! You slept with Taylor and been screwing my girl behind my back all these years—possibly being the father of her baby, and you—"

"Hold up, hold up, hold up—what you mean possibly the father? Drea', don't be coming at me outta left field with some made-up…what are you talking about?"

"I know about you and Bria hooking up all these years, and now she's pregnant, so you can't advise or tell me anything about my decision to marry Kamal or not—"

"I can when the nigga killed my cousin and got away with the shit—"

"I—Is this true, Mommy?" Tania interrupted as she stood in the hallway while her entire body began to tremble.

Ondrea then looked at Tyrin with disgust that her daughter overheard their argument. He looked down in shame, trying to avoid eye contact with the both of them. *How could I have been so stupid to not think that Tania might have been home? What did I do?!*

"Mom! Tell me cousin 'Rin is lying!" Tania screamed, filling up with rage herself. She couldn't breathe, her heart was beating one hundred miles per minute, and her palms were sweaty and turning clammy. Ondrea's reaction told Tania everything that she needed to be confirmed.

"Babygirl, I can explain—"

"I can't believe you! How can you be with a murderer…and my Daddy's murderer at that?! I never want to see, talk to, or hear from him ever again…you can't marry him, Mom!!!"

Ondrea walked over to her daughter to comfort her, but she snatched away from her grasp. "I wish it were that simple, honey, but God—"

"Don't even bring God into this; God is nowhere in this!" Tania said, "Cousin 'Rin, how long have you guys known? Is this why my Mom had stopped talking to him?"

"Yeah, baby girl," Tyrin hesitantly confirmed Tania's suspicions.

"I promise you, Mom if you marry him, you will lose me as your daughter. You can betray Dad, his life, and his memory all you want, but I can't sit back and watch you

169

do it." Tania then grabbed her car keys, got in the car, and sped off, driving aimlessly in a rage.

Ondrea then turned from the front door back over to Tyrin, "You've done enough damage... get the hell out of my house!"

"I'm not even sorry it had to go down like this, 'Drea... you know you foul for this one."

Ondrea slammed the door behind him, slid down onto the floor, and bawled her eyes out like a newborn baby. *God, please help me! Cover and protect my child while she's out driving angry. Calm her spirit, Lord, so that I can reason with her soon. Lord, please!*

****

Tyrin was beyond anger at this point. Not just with Ondrea for her decision to marry Chance's killer anyway, but because Bria was keeping something so crucial from him. **"Call me now!"** he texted.

*BRRIINNGG!!!!*

He looked at the caller ID and knew it was her. "What the hell is going on, Bria?! Do you wanna tell me the truth about this baby?"

She immediately felt like she could not breathe, like the wind was knocked out of her, and felt faint as she became highly light-headed and dizzy. *How could 'Drea tell my business?! Why did she do this?!*

"Hello, lights on, anyone home?" he demanded Bria to answer his question.

"I don't know who's baby it is, 'Rin!" she finally responded. "I don't know, okay?"

He felt instantly relieved. There was a possibility he could be a father again—and with his soulmate. Tyrin was also excited that it might be his chance at having a little "princess."

"How far along are you?"

"I don't know...a couple months, I think."

"Where are you right now?"

"No, don't even try to come and see me. Dearron is home, and I really don't wanna fool with you anymore—that's why I'm in this predicament now...I'm supposed to have a 'normal life with my husband, and like any 'normal' couple when they're pregnant, it's without a shadow of a doubt that the baby is her man's."

"But that's just it, Breeze...I am your man. You're just in denial because you're worried about what everyone would think. I didn't make you bust it open for me; you gave it up to me...you've been doing this dance with me since I was fifteen years old. Just stop, cause you know what you like—"

"That's just it, 'Rin...I like and even love what you do and who you are, but my heart is with my husband... 'D is the man God has for me."

"Yeah, aight," Tyrin retorted. "Well, make sure you call me when it's time for me to take a DNA test."

"I don't even know if I'm going to still go through with this pregnancy—"

"The hell you do! Don't kill off my possible shorty, Breeze...I mean it...think I'm playing and see what happens," his voice changed to a harsh and uncompromising tone.

"Are you threatening me?"

"I'm not gonna hurt you at all, Breeze...but I'm also not gonna allow you to kill my baby."

"You don't even know if it's your baby!" she screamed on the phone.

Tyrin's voice remained in a calm state, "Like I said, until I know for sure, you better act like you know what's good." He then hung up the phone on her.

Just then, Dearron stepped inside the guest bathroom after overhearing his wife's conversation. He wanted answers:

"So...you wanna tell me what's going on?" he asked, cool, calm, and collected.

Bria's face was as if she saw a ghost, "It-It-It's...It's not what you're thinking, babe," she stammered.

"What do you think I am thinking, dear?" he asked sarcastically.

"I don't know, but whatever it is..."

"Whatever it is? Whatever it is?! Are you kidding me?! You want me to sit up and actually believe that I did not hear you just telling another man that this baby situation you got going on isn't theirs?"

"N..N..No, that's not how the conversation went—
"

"Woman, you better quit now while you think you are ahead...so, did Taylor teach you also how to cheat on your husband, or was that just something you know how to do like you do fucking?"

Bria's tears began to pour down like torrential rain, "You don't mean that, Dearron...take that back!"

"I'm not taking anything back. I meant that shit! To think I had suspicions after I saw the way you looked at ole' boy during the engagement dinner, but no, I wanted to give you the benefit of the doubt. I wanted to believe that you wouldn't play me. Then again, once a whore, always a whore...true I couldn't turn you into no housewife."

"Fuck you, "D! You've judged me from day number one! You always had to be superior and that you were a Captain Save-a-Hoe, right?! You feel more free now that you actually acknowledged it, huh? You never stood up for me when your congregation played me! Year after year, you never backed me on not one celebration for my birthday. You never sanctioned for me to host any kind of workshops on my own, or teach any classes...and why was that, huh? Because I was never good enough in your eyes..."

"So, is that what this dude did for you? Let you feel comfortable being top-notch and not the bottom 'B?' Jezebel getting bust down out here in these streets—"

"You don't even know what you're talking about because while I was out there in those streets, that 'dude' stopped my pimp from raping me and rescued me from the life! God, you are

such a self-righteous jackass!" Bria took off running out of the house and down towards the end of their driveway.

*Raped? Pimp? Kamal said they had secrets....exactly how deep are they?* D asked himself. Immediately his heart turned back to his wife, and he felt an overwhelming sense of remorse and instantaneous forgiveness, grace, and mercy towards her. The Lord quickened him concerning his wife's past. He thanked the Holy Spirit for bringing this thought to his remembrance. While there was so much Dearron did not know about his wife, deep down, he had already made a decision to help her delve deeper into what happened. He wanted to be there for her. Not as 'Captain Save-a Hoe,' but as a husband who will love, cover, and protect his broken wife as he should.

*Lord, I come before you right now as a man who has lost his temper. Although I am beyond hurt, angry, and not even sure what the outcome of my marriage will be at this point, I am asking you first for your forgiveness for the way I talked to my wife. Secondly, I ask that you help us to get through this. In Jesus' name, I pray, Amen.*

He watched her from the foyer window. He knew they both needed their space and time. They needed to process and collect thoughts before reconvening. She was still pregnant with possibly his child—he had to make sure that she was protected.

\*\*\*\*

*I can't stand him!* Bria thought to herself as she quickly dialed Ondrea's phone. *Of course, she would have it go to voicemail...* "Ondrea, why the hell did you tell Tyrin about the baby?! D overheard me arguing with him, and now he knows! I promise Ondrea, if I wasn't pregnant, you would get these hands, trust!" Bria said and then hung up.

# Chapter Fifteen-

*God, this cannot be life! This cannot be real. There is no way You would allow me to get this close to experiencing having a dad only for it to be fake... You wouldn't do that to me, Lord, I know You wouldn't!* Tania wiped her eyes after she finished praying and proceeded to call Sincere. Until Londyn had her baby and could handle stress, Tania knew that he was the only person she could talk to that could answer her back.

"Hello," Sincere answered groggily, waking up out of deep sleep.

"Can you hold me, please?"

When he heard Tania's voice, he immediately sprung up out of bed and rushed to find clothes to put on to meet up with her. "Where are you, babe?" he asked.

"I'm—I'm …can I just come to you?" She did not

want him to know that she was parked outside of Minister

Kamal's apartment complex. She tried to catch him leaving

his apartment and confront him head-on, but she knew that

wouldn't be wise and that deep down, she wasn't ready for

that conversation.

"Um…sure…I'm still staying at my grandmother's

house in Sandy Springs…I'd feel more comfortable picking

you up, though. You sound very upset, babe, and I don't

want you driving out here this late in that condition."

Tania did not want to give up her current location,

so she told Sincere that she was at the Spring Hill Suites

hotel and hurried to that parking lot to sit. Sincere pulled up

ten minutes after her.

She ran into his already extended arms and let out

loud sobs of pain and anger. "He killed my

father…Minister Kamal killed my father, and my mom is

still going to still marry him! I don't know my father because of this man!"

"Shhh…babe, I'm sure there has to be an explanation," he said, sweeping the hair from off of her face. "Just calm down, Sweet 'T…come on, let me get you a room for the night here—are you checked in already?"

"No," she said in between sobs.

"Come on," he assured her as he grabbed her hand to escort her as they walked inside. Sincere could not believe the news he had just heard. Indeed there had to be some kind of mistake. Once they got up to Tania's room, Sincere helped her take her coat off and instructed her to lie down across the bed on her stomach. He then began to give her a massage through her clothing. "Just try and relax," he insisted.

Tania closed her eyes and surrendered to the rhythmic strokes of Sincere's hands and the James "PJ" Spraggins Pandora station he had set to play on his iPhone. Her favorite jam, "Pure Logic," began to play, and she exhaled.

"I wish I could just stay like this for eternity," she sighed.

"You can if that's really what you want..."

"I don't know what I want at this point—everything that I thought I wanted is proving to be cursed."

"Do you feel that way about us, Tania?" Sincere asked in genuine concern.

"I don't know. I know it feels like we're moving so fast, but following protocol feels like a huge joke. Nothing is ever true to script, it seems, and no one is truly one-hundred percent legit."

"So, I'm not one-hundred?"

"Don't be mad at me, but I honestly don't know who's who anymore."

"I'm sorry you feel that way, babe...I pray eventually that changes between us."

"Me too," replied Tania.

"So, where does that leave us?" he asked—his hands pausing on the small of her back.

"I don't know, Sincere...honestly, I just want to enjoy the moment."

Sincere felt defeated and decided it clearly was not the right time to propose to her. Instead, Sincere decided then that he would work harder to gain her trust since her faith had been shattered. He stopped giving her the massage and asked her to just lay in his arms as they spooned the

rest of the night.

# Chapter Sixteen-

**"9*1*1…She knows!"** Ondrea texted Kamal.

Kamal had just finished praying for daily noon
prayer and was getting ready to leave the church. *Oh, Lord.*
His heart sank. *I know she hates me now.* He then
proceeded to try and call Ondrea, but she had him on her
block list again. He then began to text Tania: **"Tania, I am
so sorry for you having to find out the way that you did
about my involvement. I am no longer that man and am
now a man of God, who has been redeemed. You HAVE
to know that I never knew your mother or that being in
love and caring for both you and her would have led us
up to this moment. I pray that you can find it in your
heart as your mother has—to one day forgive me. I
truly do love you and your mother and would love**

**nothing more than for you to have me still as your**

**'dad.' Love ya forever."**

Kamal then jumped in his SUV and headed to Ondrea's to find out what was up.

"Babe, it's me...open the door!" Kamal called out while banging on the door.

"Go away!" Ondrea shouted back through the front door. "Everything has blown up in my face...I knew I should not have decided to take you back!"

"What happened, babe? Remember what the counselor told us...we may have triggers and setbacks—"

"This ain't a damn setback, Kamal...I just may have lost my daughter behind this mess... 'Rin thinks I've betrayed their family, and on top of that...I got so angry I accidentally spilled a secret that may have cost me my best friend, too...Kamal, I just wish this never happened."

"I'm so sorry, lady," he said, sympathizing with her, "I never meant to bring you this much pain. I can't say enough how much I wish I could re-do a lot of things that I'm not proud of."

"Just, please go...I appreciate you coming to check on me, but it's just best tonight for me to have some space."

He put his hand up to the door, "Okay, lady...again, I'm so sorry."

Kamal prayed for Ondrea on his way, walking back towards his car. *Lord, keep Ondrea and hold her close. I know that all things work for Your greater good, and while I can't make any sense of this mess that I've created, I ask for relief soon. I ask for You to show Your mighty hand in this, Lord! I've asked You to do this hard thing...Lord, I release everything to You so that You can do just that. In Jesus' name, I pray, Amen.*

# Chapter Seventeen-

May 20th...Ondrea's thirty-fourth birthday, and aside from turning another year older, there was nothing to celebrate. Tania only returned back home to gather her clothes. When Sincere left to head back to college, she moved in with Bria and Dearron temporarily. It was only to be until things had the opportunity to calm down between her and her daughter. Ondrea was used to their birthday rituals of waking up to breakfast in bed, watching their favorite movie, <u>Breakfast at Tiffany's</u> together, followed by dancing to Canton Jones' "Birthday" song. *I miss my baby*, she sighed to herself.

To make matters worse, Bria wouldn't talk to her past one-word syllables, with Tania following suit. Because of Ondrea spilling the beans on Bria's pregnancy to Tyrin, she now, in a way, was forced to keep the baby. Bria didn't know how or when, but she knew eventually she would have to forgive her best friend for what she did. *Maybe this was my karma?* She often questioned herself. *This is the punishment I deserve for messing around on my husband...I have to face the consequences of my sin.* She also continued to screen and block Tyrin's calls and text messages. *I need to just change my number.*

****

Kamal tried his best to respect Ondrea's boundaries. He wanted to help her celebrate her birthday, but she said that she still was not ready to enjoy his company while her daughter felt how she felt about the whole ordeal. *She did well enough to just come to church to still hear The Word,* he reminded himself. He prepared himself to address the congregation:

"Praise the Lord, Saints, I'd like to start off by wishing my fiancee', Ms. Ondrea Williams, a very Happy Birthday this morning."

"Happy Birthday!" Some of the members called out, clapped, and whistled in approval. At the same time, she smiled uncomfortably and waved hello to the congregation. *He tried it,* she thought to herself—somewhat flattered. She then smiled back at Kamal.

"Now, I'd like to call your attention to 1 John 2:20 & 21...it reads 'But ye have an unction from the Holy One, and ye know all things. I have not written unto you because ye know not the truth, but because ye know it, and that no lie is of the truth.' My subject is taken from this verse. The author, Kimberla Lawson-Roby, is: 'Thoughts, Ideas and Suggestions...' You see, when we become Christians, Christ's Spirit is something we receive. Through Christ's Spirit is how truth is communicated to us and hearing the

Word from leaders according to His heart and while praying and fasting. When we do all of these things, it clears the path for God to speak to us through our thoughts, which in turn, become our ideas."

"Alright now, Pastor!" Mrs. Turner shouted out.

"Also, 1 Corinthians 2:16 states 'For who hath known the mind of the Lord, that he may instruct him? But we have the mind of Christ.' When God saves and renews our minds, He starts thinking His thoughts through us, which helps us align ourselves with His will. Philippians

2:13 says, 'For it is God which worketh in You both to Will and to do His good pleasure.' This means that God can direct your will and create a desire in you to do what pleases Him. Now, it's better to have a willing mind, but how many of you know when God gets through with you, He's gonna get His glory anyhow?"

"You're talking right, preacher!" a visitor yelled out, along with a couple of "Amen's" and "Glory's."

"One way to know it's probably God's will is when the desire keeps on reappearing. This is why it's crucial to monitor and screen thoughts that we may entertain to make sure they line up with His will, not the devil's plan. The enemy comes to steal, kill, and destroy, but Church, we already know he is defeated."

"You better teach, sir!"

"Because he has no authority over death and he cannot act in his own authority and force us to do anything, the devil can only suggest things. Luke 6:45 tells us to guard our hearts. The latter clause says, '...for of the abundance of the heart his mouth speaketh...' and with this being said, Saints, this is why it's important to know Satan monitors our words and studies our hearts...this is why death and life are in the power of your tongue...he is the father of lies. James 3:15 says, 'This wisdom descendeth not from above, but is earthly, sensual, and devilish...so, there are three ways that you can tell Satan's tactics to try and get you out there so he can knock your head off."

At this moment, you could hear a pin drop...everyone was all ears to what the Spirit had to say.

"Number one: It feels like your own idea—like for example, a couple thinking *'wouldn't it be great not to have to go through this situation?'* and they divorce...this could lead to the both of them being out of His will because they weren't comfortable with whatever they had to go through together. Number two: the suggestion is filled with questions that cause you to doubt the original thought— also known as overthinking. For example, when we think long, we start to think wrong... *'Did God really say that to me? Is it really a sin?'* Just like the serpent tempted Eve in the Garden of Eden. She knew what God had told her because she and Adam heard Him audibly. Still, the enemy came and planted those seeds of doubt in her. His job was to cause her to be used to not only throw herself out of God's will for her life, but she even messed up the man who God gave her to be a helpmate...she helped him, alright...to God's judgment."

"Jesus!"

"Which leads us to Number three: This is where you have to watch out for those friends and family and the environments we place ourselves in. The friends and family that will always side with you no matter what. The type that when you're trying to fight against temptation, they say something like, *'I wouldn't worry about that...or 'no time is better than right now.'* So, I'll leave you with this—1 Peter 5:8 says, 'Be sober, be vigilant, because your adversary the devil, as a roaring lion, walketh about seeking whom he may devour.' The only way to be sober-minded is having first the willing mind to seek Christ and His will daily, hourly, by the minute….the second…"

"Preach!"

"Having our armor on, consecrated, and prayed up is the only way!"

"Hallelujah!"

****

"Great sermon, Minister," said Ondrea. "And thanks for the birthday shout-out...I got dealt with during your sermon. Even though I decided to move forward with you, I can't lie that I know it was God telling me to do so. Mother Helen also had some words of revelation for me."

"I appreciate that lady, but God gets the glory for this message. I only say it as He gives it to me."

"Well, have a good rest of the day…"

"What are you getting into today?" Kamal asked, cutting her off.

"Nothing really. I'm just gonna take myself out to the movies and veg out on pizza and ice cream."

"Well, let me know if you want any company."

"Thanks, but no thanks, Kamal…I just want to be prayerful and have no distractions while I contemplate how I want to handle our future."

"While I don't like the idea, I have to respect it…again, Happy Birthday, babe," he said as he gave her a sweet hug and kissed her on the cheek.

"Thanks again," Ondrea stated sincerely.

Kamal smiled as he watched Ondrea walk outside the Sanctuary. This time around, this setback was not as torturous as the last, where there was no contact or communication at all. He trusted God's process before and would be patient this time around and see it through. He also wished that Tania would hear him out, but ever since she found out about what he did, she had no words for him.

# Chapter Eighteen-

Tania missed her mother, but she could not understand why she still was okay with marrying Minister Kamal. This was the first birthday that she did not give her mother the usual breakfast in bed and follow their tradition. Her party that she was supposed to have for her

"Why don't you text her if you don't want to call her?" Bria asked. Even though she was conflicted in her feelings, she knew that Ondrea was miserable without her daughter. Bria definitely didn't want the wedge between Tania and her mother to have anything to do with her.

"I guess you're right," Tania agreed. She picked up her phone to send her a text: **"Happy Birthday, Mommy. No matter what, I still love you. Enjoy your special day."**

"I'm proud of you, Tania. Thanks for doing that for your mother."

"What about you, God Mommy? Have you texted or called her?"

"Actually, I sent her a text message also, Taniecey-Pooh. They're probably just now getting out of service, so I don't expect her to check her phone until then...oh, did 'D tell you Treasure is here?"

"No, ma'am," Tania said, surprised. "I thought that she wouldn't be home for another month?"

"Dane told us that her mother had to go on another assignment overseas, so she had to come now."

Treasure was their seventeen-year-old niece who grew quite fond of Tania when she had spent the night the last time she was visiting her father and Dearron's twin

brother, Dane. She was a little eccentric and spontaneous,

but she was a straight "A" student and had no babies or did

drugs to anyone's knowledge. Tania couldn't wait to hang

with her.

****

*BRRRIINGG!!!*

"Hey, girl!"

"Oh, hey T! I heard you're staying in town for a lil'

minute…"

"Yeah, a lot of drama back at home with my mom

and her murderer/preacher/hubby…what are you doing

later?" asked Tania

"Let's rewind the question back first to your mom's 'murderer/preacher/hubby'… I mean, what's that all about?"

"Why did I find out that her fiance' was the one who had something to do with my Dad being murdered?"

"Shut the front door!" Treasure couldn't believe what she was hearing. "Girl, that's heavy...what did your Mom say about it? Has he said anything to you?"

"He texted me, I guessed when he knew I had found out, but I'm not trying to hear anything from no one right now, you know?"

"I guess...girl, I would at least hear them out instead of being left to my own thoughts. It may not have gone down as you think—then again, it could have—but at least your mind can rest in knowing the truth…"

"It sounds so cliche, but I don't think I can handle the truth," Tania admitted.

"The truth makes us free, though…"

"Okay, so now you're all in the scriptures?"

"I didn't know that was in the 'Good Book,' so maybe God is trying to tell you something, and that 'something is to hear them out so you can be free."

"I hear you…I was gonna try and have a movie night with my God Mommy, but since you're in town, I don't want to miss out," Tania replied, changing the subject.

"Good choice, chica!" Treasure said as she applied

her lip shine from Neda's Natural Beauty. "My boy, Reg is having a party tonight, and you gotta roll with me."

"Alright," Tania said, "just let me know what time I need to be ready."

"Seven P.M. is good for me!"

"I'll be ready!"

**** 

Tania was so excited for the night and was seductively cute in a blue DKNY sundress. Once Treasure picked her up, she had no questions until they pulled up to a random house.

"What's this?" she asked nervously.

"Reg throws parties here sometimes...you're not scared, are you?"

"N—no," Tania lied.

Once they arrived inside the house, Treasure gave Tania a red cup with some punch in it. "Drink some of this...it'll help you relax."

"I—I don't know, Treasure..."

"Come on, girl...have I steered you wrong yet?"

"No." Tania took a sip of the punch and made a face of discomfort. "This is nasty! This tastes like a weird tea!" she added.

"You have to keep drinking it, and after a while, it won't be so bad..." She didn't bother to tell her the "tea" was a mixture of alcohol and the new "it" tea, BLK Sapote.

"I guess," Tania said as she braced herself to drink the rest. At that point, she did not care anymore.

"Who's this baddie?" Treasure's friend Reg asked her as he came up and slid his arm around her.

"This is my girl, T...it's her first time, so be gentle."

"Are you gonna get one?" he asked her.

"What is he talking about, Treasure?" Tania asked nervously.

Treasure interrupted Tania, "He's talking about a tattoo...he does them also at these parties...anyways, I want a butterfly one."

Tania had never experienced 'walking on the wild side.' Still, after the past week that she had had, she was open to anything.

"I'd like to get something on my shoulder with my father—"

"Are you serious, T?" Treasure asked. "You know there's no pressure to get one."

"I know...this is something that I need to do for me," she stated. "As I was saying, I'd like to get my father's face with 'Love always your daddy's girl' written underneath it...I have his pic in my phone."

"Alrighty then... Reg, hook her up," Treasure directed as she got another red cup with a punch, downed it, and proceeded to get on top of one of the tables and dance wildly.

The sounds of cheering and cat-calling came from numerous young males in the room as they watched Treasure dance. Tania continued to follow Reg in the backroom for her first tattoo. It hurt badly, but about two hours later, she could not help but smile at the results on her left shoulder.

"For your first time, you've been a trooper, Lil' Mama," he said to her.

"Thanks again, Reg...I'm glad that I came...no pain, no gain, right? Now, where can I find Treasure?" she asked as he escorted her from the back.

"She is probably booed up with her dude...he's in here…over there," Reg pointed over at the two of them in the corner, making out.

"What the hell?!" Tania said in shock, as she saw the top of Treasure's dude's hair—a man bun!" *No, no, no...I know that's not who I think it is!* Tania marched over towards the couple. "Sebastian?!"

He looked startled, "T-T-Tania...I-I," he stuttered.

"Wow, 'playboy,'" she said with the words seething through her teeth. "So, how long has this been going on?"

"Wait, you know him?!" Treasure asked.

"Know him? He was my boyfriend, and I almost let him take my virginity...I'm glad I gave it to someone else!"

"You what?!" Sebastian said with surprise following anger, "But you—"

Treasure then turned back to Sebastian. "Forget that part, Sebastian! Tell her how long we've been fooling around!" she demanded.

Sebastian's face, already beet-red, began to become pale, "Well...I've been going with Treasure for about six months..."

"But, what about all the time you spent with me? When did you guys hook up?!"

"Girl, his aunt lives down the street from me, so that's how we would see each other whenever he and his parents came over...you bastard...I can't believe you played us like this!"

Treasure exclaimed as she smacked him across the face.

"I hate you!" Tania screamed as she ran out of the house and took off down the street.

"Hold up, Tania!" Sebastian yelled as he chased her down the street.

" 'F' you, Sebastian!" Tania yelled back. She ran at full speed ahead...tears hot and trailing down her cheeks to the point she became blinded by them. She didn't look up in time to see a Dodge Ram turn the corner and plowed right into her,

sending her body flying into the air and landing an entire

mile away.

"Tania! No, baby!" Sebastian cried out as he

kneeled down to check and see if she had a pulse. "Call 9-

1-1!!! Somebody, please call for help, please! God, please

help her!"

# Chapter Nineteen-

There was an awkward silence in the emergency waiting room. Sebastian, Dane, Treasure, Bria, and Dearron were all in attendance as they waited for Kamal to drive Ondrea down. There was no way that he would let her drive in the current mental and emotional state that she was in. Sebastian had reached out to 'T but made him promise not to tell Londyn yet because he didn't want to bring extra stress on Londyn, who had two more months to go before Journey Diane would be born.

You could feel the tension in the air when Tyrin and T arrived in the waiting room.

"Lord, hold my peace and my tongue!" D stated aggressively as he looked straight at Tyrin.

"Yeah, you better pray—"

"This is not the time, nor the place for this, guys...seriously!" Bria pleaded at the same time that the doctor entered the room. Tania had been in recovery from an emergency three-hour surgery.

"Doc, how is my Goddaughter doing?" Dearron rushed to ask. Both he and Bria thanked God that Ondrea had them as emergency contacts and POAs in all of her and Tania's paperwork.

The doctor's face grew more serious. He stalled a little for time, then began to speak, "She's suffered extensive damage to her skull, lungs, upper and lower torsos and has broken both of her legs and pelvis. We have her heavily sedated and in a semi-coma just until the swelling of her brain comes down a little."

"Oh, God, no!" Bria called out as Dearron caught her mid-fall.

"Can we see her?" Sebastian asked.

"Please, you're the last person she'd wanna see!" Treasure retorted.

"Alright, everyone, just calm down," Dane stated. "If anyone sees her first, it should be her mother when she gets here...agreed?"

"Agreed," Sebastian replied.

****

"My baby..." Ondrea's voice trailed off as she looked out of the window in Kamal's Cadillac SUV, "...this is all my fault, you know..."

"Lady, this is not your fault...if anyone is to blame, I will take full responsibility. Let's continue to remember that God is in control. No matter what we find out when we get down there, just know that our ways are not His and that He has begun a good work in Tania...she'll pull through because her time is not finished."

Kamal reached over to hold Ondrea's hand. She squeezed his hand back firmly...he could feel the overwhelming presence of worry and fear consuming her at that moment.

"Dear Lord, we come to You humbly...thanking You for watching over us throughout this day and keeping us in this hour. We ask for traveling mercies as we make our way to Savannah to see about our daughter, Tania. Lord, we give our worries and fear surrounding the unknown to You and rejoice in advance for all you will do in the future. It is so. In Jesus' name, Amen."

# Chapter Twenty-

Once inside and three more hours later, Ondrea knew she was about to face yet another hard blow. Just for her to look around the waiting room, and with both Bria and Dearron, Dane, Treasure, Sebastian, 'T and Tyrin all present, she knew it could not be good. After she was informed of Tania's condition, Kamal escorted her to Tania's bedside.

"Oh my, baby!" she screamed as she looked upon her daughter's badly bruised body and swollen face.

Tyrin swallowed his pride and rushed into the room for assistance, "You want me to take her out, dude?"

Kamal looked up in surprise at Tyrin addressing him since the last encounter back in February, "Hey…uh, sure...I'm just going to pray over Tania real quick...gotta do that..."

Tyrin's tone softened, "True dat...we gotta pray and come together for Baby Girl at this time. I can pick the beef up at a later date, but I'm gone need you to do that preacher-reverend-pastor magic that you do."

Kamal smiled and extended his hand for the truce, "I got you, sir...but it's God who gets all His glory," he added. Tyrin shook his hand in agreement and escorted Ondrea over to a chair where she could sit down. "Dear Heavenly Father, we stand before you knowing that all power is in Your hands. That same resurrection power that raised Your son, Jesus, in three days, is the very same resurrecting power that can heal all of our baby girl, Tania. Lord, we know that she still has more work to do here while on Earth, and we know that she has had a very rough life with a lot of things happening to her that she may never understand nor feel peace about. Lord, I ask as Your manservant if I am any way pleasing in Your sight that You supernaturally heal Tania's body from the inside out. We are thankful for the guidance and wisdom that You have given everyone who is caring for her while she is here and thank You in advance for the positive outlook on her condition. She will wake up in Jesus' name in her right mind! She will wake up in Jesus' name, with the activities of her limbs! She will wake up in Jesus' name with a testimony like none other! When other young people see her and hear it, they will have no choice but to bow down and worship You! Please comfort Ondrea, Lord…please, don't take anything else away from her! Lord, in Your name, You were in the process of restoring the years that had been stolen from Ondrea. Continue to perform that for her until the day of Your return—whether here on Earth or in the air. Let there be peace for this family in the midst the process and journey in Tania's healing. In Jesus' name, we pray, Amen, Amen, and it is so."

When Kamal finished praying for Tania, God's presence could definitely be felt in the room. There was not a dry eye in sight. Ondrea remained seated in the chair next to her bedside, while the others had quietly filed in the room at some point during the prayer.

"Minister Kamal, that was an awesome prayer. I'm sure God heard it," Bria said, thanking him with a hearty hug.

"Yeah, bro...Amen, and Amen!" exclaimed Dearron.

"I got your text, Dad...I forgive you," a faint whisper came from Tania, who was starting to wake up.

"Doc! Doc! She's waking up!" Dearron rushed out of the room to get the doctor that was on call.

"Tania, my baby!" Ondrea cried tears of joy.

Kamal stood speechless at the mighty hand of God and the supernatural wonder that He had just performed, "Oh, baby girl...I thank God you know I'm not that same person. I am so deeply sorry that I took the most precious person from you. Lord, I praise You in advance for restoration and healing on the inside and outside...spiritually and mentally...Lord, I thank You!" he said while holding Tania's hand. "Now, get some rest, baby girl...you have to save that strength for your recovery," he added as she managed a smile and closed her eyes once more for rest.

****

"I guess I'll get 'T on back up North in the morning...thanks again, man, for that prayer. I know God is with you now," Tyrin said to Kamal.

"For the record—"

"Baby steps, my dude—"

"No, I owe you this... I'm very sorry from the bottom of my heart, and I'm not that man anymore. I pray one day after Tania is fully recovered that you can find it in your heart not to pick the beef back up, but can forgive me."

Tyrin did not know how to respond to Kamal's apology but instead just nodded his head in agreement, "I hear you," was all he said.

# Chapter Twenty One-

"So, what brings you three in today?" asked Pastor Samuels, Kamal's spiritual father in the gospel and current Pastor of Destiny to Faith Deliverance. Usually, he never counseled after service unless it was emergent. However, when he received the text from Minister Kamal, Pastor Samuels knew there should be some urgency since he never contacted him last-minute to meet.

"I'll start," Kamal began, "First off, I thank you for agreeing to meet with all of us after Tania was finally released from the rehab facility."

"It's no problem, my son. I knew it had to be serious and definitely wanted to do it while Tania feels up to it...How are you doing, young lady?" Pastor Samuels asked as he looked at Tania sitting in her wheelchair. It had been a long and strenuous three-month battle. She went through intensive inpatient physical and occupational therapy during rehab. With just six more months and one more surgery, she should be ready for a cane.

"I'm feeling much better, Pastor...I'm learning to take everything one day at a time. If it was not for these two, I don't know what I would do or where I'd be. I truly thank God for another chance."

"That's the best medicine, my dear...and always remember what He's done for you...All Right Minister, you can continue..."

"Yes, sir...well, some years ago...way before I accepted the call to ministry on my life, I was involved in selling drugs. During that time, there was a rival drug dealer with who I had a misunderstanding, and as a result, it ended up in his murder."

Tears began to fall from both Ondrea and Tania's eyes.

Kamal continued with his confession, "I had no idea that man would be Ondrea's husband and Tania's father. I had no clue until after I had proposed to her, and we were five months before this wedding."

"I see..." Pastor Samuels pondered.

"So, as you can see, this is, in fact, a hard situation for all of us to work through...I love both of them and want nothing more than to still move forward with our wedding in November...I just don't know how to do that, and if the two of them are sure to try and move forward with me on this journey."

"Ondrea?" Pastor Samuels solicited her input.

She hesitated. "Although this man has caused my daughter and me so much grief, I cannot lie and say that he has not made up for that hurt and had an intricate part in my healing process up until learning this news...Pastor, I honestly don't know how to proceed although, I do love him."

"Tania?" Pastor Samuels continued his assessment.

"I don't understand a lot of things. I'm pissed, hurt, and upset at the both of them for falling in love with each other. I'm like, *'why do I have to go through something like this?'* I mean, how can I look this man in the face every day knowing that he's responsible for me, never knowing my father? I mean, some days I am good, and the others, I want to never see him again in my life."

"Tania, all of your feelings are valid and realistic," Pastor Samuels stated. "Kamal is right...this is a tough situation; however, we serve a God who says to 'ask Him a hard thing!' If He can't do anything else, one thing we know He cannot do is lie. His truth will reign supreme over anything spoken against this union or the plans and thoughts that God has concerning you three and more children to come...stay prayerful. I want to continue to meet with you three weekly. Tania, on the rough days, you can join via Zoom, and we'll go from there...Oh my, when you get finished growing through this...God will get ALL the glory!!!"

"Thank you, Pastor," Kamal stated. "We appreciate you."

"Anytime, my son...remember, 1 Corinthians 13:4-8...the greatest message preached through your union is that 'Love Never Fails.'"

# Epilogue (Thanksgiving Day)-

"Your moment is here 'Drea...you ready?" Tyrin asked as he prepared to walk her down the aisle to give her away in marriage to Pastor Kamal Davis. Ondrea never thought that Tyrin could get to this point in the forgiveness of his cousin's murderer; however, God had done such a miraculous work in not just his life but also the lives of everyone attached to them.

Ondrea smiled and nodded as she locked arms with Tyrin and started their walk towards the sanctuary when they heard the song "This Very Moment" by K-Ci & Jo Jo. As the french doors opened, everyone stood as she and Tyrin entered the sanctuary. Ondrea could hear the "ooh's and aah's" as the congregation, family, and friends admired her iconic peach-colored Vera Wang mermaid gown.

The sanctuary was beautifully decorated in the bride and groom's colorful theme with a mixture of the colors gray, champagne, gold, burgundy, and salmon. Standing alongside Kamal was Dearron, his Best Man, and Bria, Ondrea's Matron of Honor. Tania was there, looking radiant in her blinged-out wheelchair, with her and Londyn as her mother's Maid of Honor and Jr. Bridesmaid, with Marie as a Bridesmaid. Aunt Shelby sat right up in the front next to a date she had brought to the wedding.

"Who gives this woman to be married?" Pastor Samuels began once Tyrin, and Ondrea made their way up to the altar.

"I do," Tyrin said with a smile. He dapped Kamal and stepped to the side as he claimed his bride.

"If anyone finds just cause that these two should not be together, please speak now, or forever hold your peace…"

Suddenly, sudden cries from Journey Diane rang out. T quickly stepped over both Sebastian and Sincere to excuse himself and her to see if she needed a diaper change or a bottle. While everyone's attention was on T and the baby, Tania couldn't help but meet Sebastian's gaze. She quickly looked away in the moment of awkwardness.

"Alright now, little baby," Pastor Samuels joked as everyone chuckled. "Anyone else? Going once...going twice..."

After the solos were sung and scriptures read, it was time for the nuptials. They both had written their own vows:

"With this ring, I vow to love you as Christ loves His church. I vow to honor you in sickness and health, good and the bad, happy and sad, lol..." more chuckles from the congregation filled the room. "No, but in all seriousness, I never knew the depth of love unconditionally until I met and have been on this journey with you. The things that you know about me did not deter you from still wanting to be with me. No—no matter how hard it was to hear and imagine...and for that, I know without a shadow of a doubt that God has joined us together. Through your love, He has given me grace, mercy, and unmerited favor. I have found my 'good thing' and do not plan on ever letting you go. I love you, Ondrea Brenae." When Kamal finished, again, there wasn't a dry eye in sight—not even his own.

After wiping her eyes with one of her gloves, Ondrea followed, "With this ring, I vow to be a helpmate to you and support you as the man of God that I know you to be. You have embraced my daughter as if she was your very own and have shown me the power of God's Spirit. You've done this not just when I hear you while you're bringing forth God's Word, but

When you came into my life and helped me get free of all of the hurt, pain, heaviness, and depression that was weighing me down. I thank you for speaking life into me, even though it looked as if you had been involved with the death. Life followed after, and for that, I thank God. You are food for my soul, and I know without a shadow of a doubt that you are the covering and man that God made specifically for me in this time, this space, and for the rest of my life here on Earth. I love you, Kamal Anthony Davis, with all my heart and soul."

After communion and singing of the Lord's prayer by the powerful singer Autumn Joy Lee-Cass, Pastor Samuels finished the marriage ceremony:

"We have witnessed this union by joining hands, giving in rings, and communion following vows. And now by the power vested in me by God and the State of Georgia,

I pronounce you two husband and wife...you may now kiss your bride!"

As Kamal and Ondrea kissed passionately—for all that they had been through—all that they had endured, love won!

**GOD NEVER FAILS!!!!**

**\*\*\*\***

**Join Love Series Email List!!!!**

**Beautyfromashesllc44@gmail.com**

**Follow For Updates!!!!!**

**Website: beautyfromashes44.com**

**FB**: @theloveseries44

**IG**: authorcarriefarley

**Twitter**: FarleyCarrie

**Previous Books:**

*Love Chances*

*Love Changes*